MIA

Dreams
Do
Come
True

MIA CARUSO

BALBOA
PRESS

A DIVISION OF HAY HOUSE

Balboa Press books may be ordered through booksellers or by contacting:

Balboa Press
A Division of Hay House
1663 Liberty Drive
Bloomington, IN 47403
www.balboapress.com
1 (877) 407-4847

Because of the dynamic nature of the Internet, any web addresses or links contained in this book may have changed since publication and may no longer be valid. The views expressed in this work are solely those of the author and do not necessarily reflect the views of the publisher, and the publisher hereby disclaims any responsibility for them.

The author of this book does not dispense medical advice or prescribe the use of any technique as a form of treatment for physical, emotional, or medical problems without the advice of a physician, either directly or indirectly. The intent of the author is only to offer information of a general nature to help you in your quest for emotional and spiritual well-being. In the event you use any of the information in this book for yourself, which is your constitutional right, the author and the publisher assume no responsibility for your actions.

Any people depicted in stock imagery provided by Thinkstock are models, and such images are being used for illustrative purposes only. Certain stock imagery © Thinkstock.

Print information available on the last page.

ISBN: 978-1-5043-3723-6 (sc)
ISBN: 978-1-5043-3725-0 (hc)
ISBN: 978-1-5043-3724-3 (e)

Library of Congress Control Number: 2015912360

Balboa Press rev. date: 08/27/2015

Contents

CHAPTER 1

JP

A s far back as I can remember, I was a dreamer—not just any dreamer. I was born to dream; it was the one thing in life that I did well. I can remember being in elementary school and not being able to concentrate because of my incessant dreaming. I lived in a world of fantasy, which I thought was normal until I got older and realized I was by myself.

Everyone I knew went off to school, got married, or got a job. They were planning their futures like normal people do, and I was not. I was waiting for "the one" to walk into my life. Not just any "one." Mine was special. I know this might sound a little crazy, but he and I were together before this lifetime. It was not about falling in love with someone; it was much deeper. He and I were bonded together for all eternity, etched into each other's hearts and souls forever. There would be no "death do us part." Growing up, I honestly felt as though I was an alien who was dropped off on this planet and that in the process of being dropped off, he and I were separated. Now my sole mission in life was to find him. Sort of like a twin without the other half. A part of me was definitely missing.

Like a ship without an anchor, my mind would drift to wherever my fantasy world of thoughts would take me, floating away in search of my true love. Unfortunately, since my mind would drift off so frequently, it was difficult for me to have a conversation with someone. My mind would wander away into my dream world, searching for him. This was a very annoying trait, but those who knew me accepted my rude manner. Those who did not know me probably thought I was a flake. It was rude. I hated how my mind operated, because I was constantly thinking of him. I was desolate without him.

Everyone has a purpose or a passion in life, and this was mine. I knew he was out there waiting for me and that as soon as our eyes met—like magic—we would instantly know who the other person was. Finally, my heart would be home again. God only knows how badly I wanted to be home! This was the reason I was born, my absolute reason for living. I never shared this thought with anyone. I kept it to myself like a well-guarded secret, safe within my heart. I was just waiting for the day my true love would appear so we could be together forever. I just wanted to go home, and he was my home.

Although he didn't have a certain look—like blond hair and blue eyes or dark hair and dark eyes—I knew he would have a certain look in his eyes. I would know him immediately. I would talk to God and say, "Hello, uh, excuse me, God. Where did my heart go—my true love? He's not with me. Is this some sort of joke? If it is, it's not funny."

As I got older, about the time all my friends went off to plan their futures and left me behind, I realized I had to dismiss my dreams and grow up. I started to feel I had let my dreams get the better of me. I decided my thoughts about true love were just some fantasy I had concocted as a young child, like some sort of Cinderella story. I somehow convinced myself that he didn't exist; it was a childhood fairy tale I had to forget.

Fast-forward to my life now. I was in the kitchen, washing dishes while looking out the window, wondering what my life was missing. I had a wonderful husband who loved me, great kids, a beautiful home—what else could I need or want? What was wrong with me? The feelings I had when I was young were coming back again. The wanting, the need for something more, the emptiness that had not been filled deep within my soul. *I know passion is lacking in my relationship, but so what? Everyone is so busy; who has time for romance and all that stuff? Right? Wrong!*

I fantasized all the time about being swept away with romance. I dreamed of my Prince Charming treating me like Cinderella or of a man seducing me just by looking at me. I'd run the gamut of emotions: fantasy, love, lust, seduction, and crushes—playing everything out in my mind.

One day while having lunch with a friend, I told her about the emptiness I was feeling. I did not mention all the fantasizing. Life is about real issues—money, bills, work, kids, relationships—and we have to tackle whatever problems surface on any given day. That is reality, not my make-believe fantasy life. It was time for me to figure out what was missing in my life.

Much to my surprise, my friend was feeling the same way, although she'd never said anything to me until this day. I guess some things we keep to ourselves. She said that sometimes she falls asleep and dreams of things that she wants in her life—and they become real in her dreams. Whatever she is yearning for at that moment comes alive through her dreams. My first thought was, *does she know who she is talking to?* I mean, after all, I was born to dream, but I'd never imagined myself getting caught up in my dreams again, not like this, anyhow!

That night in bed, I allowed my mind to wander to wherever it wanted to go. At some point, I felt as though my body was drifting up and away. I felt like my spirit had been set free. I had a thin, cotton, strapless dress wrapped around my chest and draped down to the middle of my thighs. My hair was flowing wildly with a flower tucked on one side. I was standing near a lagoon on a very beautiful tropical island, surrounded by palm trees and soft white sand. The water was crystal clear. I had never seen such beauty until I looked up and saw him. He had perfect body; he looked like he had been chiseled out of stone. His bronze tan glistened in the sunlight.

I could feel the passion building inside of me. The sun was starting to set, and the sky began to change from sky blue to pink. As we walked toward each other, our eyes locked. The passion inside of me was ready to burst. His eyes were a seductive, deep black. I found myself sucked in by his trance, and my body was screaming with an intense, powerful pulsing. Shock waves rippled throughout my body as our hands touched. The electricity was flowing, and my mind was racing with a million thoughts and emotions. I was hoping that my feelings of elation were not apparent on my face. I was trying to be cool—like it happened to me all the time!

With a soft, sexy voice, he said, "I'm Kane."

I said, "I'm Rayne."

He asked how long I was going to be on the island because he would love to give me a private tour.

We started walking. For some reason, I had a strong feeling that I had known him all my life. I felt oddly comfortable, like we were one. He took me to see a volcano that had been dormant for more than one hundred years, which sounded like a long time, but isn't a very long time in volcano years. The moon and the stars lit up the sky as he turned and looked at me. His eyes were speaking to my soul. I didn't want to look away. I had waited for that moment my whole life.

When he wrapped his arms around me, I could feel his strong body up against mine. My heart was pounding out of control. I had never felt that way. I did not know how to stop my heart from beating. I sensed he felt the same way. He began to caress my body; his lips were soft as they moved all around my face and neck. I wanted him so badly I was quivering at the thought of him being inside of me. I could not believe that we were actually making love; it was one of those moments you try to hold on to because you know how special it is. I did not want him to let me go. I had never felt so safe and loved. *Don't let me go.*

When we were done, he whispered in my ear, "There is something else I want you to see." I was aching for his arms to be wrapped around me as he took my hand and led me to the small village where he'd grown up. They were having some kind of celebration. He told me the luau was a tradition in his culture. Torches outlined the perimeter of the luau, lighting up the party. They had cooked whole pigs that were displayed as centerpieces. They had pineapples, coconut cups, and flowers of every color around their necks. The women also wore flowers in their hair. Everyone was hula dancing.

Kane explained how the hula was very different between the men and the women. For women, the hula was a very sensual swaying to the beat of the music, telling a story like sign language. The male hula dancer was more aggressive in his style, reflecting his warrior spirit. Everything seemed so primitive; I felt like I was back in another time period. The evening went by so fast I could not believe when it was over! As Kane walked me back to the lagoon, I kept thinking, *I hope this is not a dream.*

When I woke, I could see the morning sunlight coming through my bedroom window. I was saddened by the idea that it was only a dream; it seemed so real. I'd never had a dream that touched me so deeply. I just wanted to stay in bed and be with Kane. I tried to let the dream go, but I could not. For some reason, it was like a recording in my mind that would not stop. I decided to do some research to see what island I might have been on. It appeared that I must have been there during a more primitive time because the clothes, the village, and the landscape were not of this day and age.

The dream seemed so real, though. Kane seemed so real. Why can't I stop thinking about him?

Chapter 2

I wanted to get on with my day so I could hurry and get back to Kane. I did my usual routine—I dropped the kids off at school, ran errands, cleaned up the house, did laundry, picked the kids up from school, and prepared dinner. It was much more exciting than usual, though. I couldn't stop thinking about Kane. My mind kept drifting back to the island. It was so beautiful, and everything had happened so fast. It was magical! I wanted to see him again—I needed to see him again.

I couldn't believe what a hold this dream had on me. It was just a dream, but it couldn't have been more real. I felt as though I was living a double life, and it was hard to determine what was real and what was not. At dinner, my husband said I was acting differently. I really didn't know what to say. *Oh, honey. I had a dream about this gorgeous man named Kane. I think I'm in love.* Instead I just said, "Oh," and I asked him about his day.

Meanwhile, I was counting the minutes before bedtime. I thought it would be difficult getting to sleep. Surprisingly, I felt myself going into a deep slumber. I awoke to find myself on a train, which startled me at first because I expected to be on a tropical island. I immediately noticed I wasn't on Amtrak. I heard someone say Dr. Deutsche Reichsbahn. The train was black and

7

white as well as everything else. Even the people were dressed in black and white. There was no color. Everything appeared very drab. Everyone wore uniforms and was speaking a different language. It sounded like German. What was strange was that I could understand everything—and I didn't speak German! My hair and my clothes were different too. By the looks of things, I think it was around the time of World War II. I knew I would just have to see where this dream took me.

As the train began to slow down and come to a stop, a strikingly gorgeous, tall, blond-haired, blue-eyed man quickly took a seat on the aisle beside me. *Oh my God. You are so gorgeous.*

He leaned over and whispered, "Pretend you are with me. I'm going to lay my head on your shoulder." So many things were running through my head. I wondered if he had a gun. I knew it was a dream, but I did not know if he was going to kill me! It all happened so fast. I did not have time to react. I saw men in uniforms with serious, intimidating looks on their faces walking forcefully through the train. I breathed a sigh of relief as they went to the next train car.

When it was safe, he sat up and said, "I am Wieland." He thanked me for the cover and explained he was there on business.

So what if he is strikingly beautiful? I should have gotten up and left, but I could not. Something inside of me was telling me to stay. Wieland asked me where I was from and how long I would be staying. I told him I was looking for a hotel in town. He gave me the name of his hotel: Hotel Wittelsbach. As the train came to a stop, he said, "This is where you want to get off for the Hotel Wittelsbach."

The wind was starting to pick up, and it looked as though there was going to be a snowstorm. While I was waiting for a cab, my dress was blowing uncontrollably in the wind. I think he realized I needed some help getting a cab.

Once he hailed me a cab, he told the driver where to take me. As we were pulling away, he asked my name. I told him. I was excited that we would be staying in the same hotel, but I wondered when Kane was going to show up.

The hotel was very close to the train station, which was convenient after the long train ride. When we arrived, I noticed a quaint three-story Bavarian-style hotel nestled into a small ski town. It was a very beautiful sight.

The cab driver said this was the village of Oberammergau. The village was surrounded by the Bavarian Alps. I could not help but wonder why I was there. *Where is my lagoon? Where is Kane?* I was going to look around town to see if I ran into anyone. Since this was a dream, I found thousands of dollars of Deutschemarks, the German currency, in my purse along with my passport. I was set. *So what else is a girl to do with money in her pocket and time on her hands? Shop!*

While shopping, I heard a lot of buzz about *The Passion Play*. When I returned to the hotel, I knew I would have to inquire about how to obtain tickets for it. After a couple of hours of shopping, I decided to go back to the hotel, freshen up, and find something to eat. The restaurant in the hotel looked like the perfect spot to have a nice, quiet meal.

I could not figure out this dream. *Why am I here?* I ordered a beer and bratwurst for dinner, and I noticed the mood of everyone. They seemed like they were let down in some way, and the air had a gloomy, depressed feeling. I knew there was a war going on, but this was different.

I asked the waiter what was going on, and he told me *The Passion Play* had been canceled due to the war. I asked him why it was so disappointing if it was just a play. He said *The Passion Play*, which the town was known for, started in 1633 when soldiers returning home after the Thirty Years' War brought the Black Death with them. They did not realize the bacillus *Yersinia pestis* was spread by the fleas, which was carried by the rats that accompanied the soldiers. The people of Oberammergau tried to prevent the plague from entering their village. They closed the village so no one could enter. Unfortunately, the plague caught up to them, and as a last effort to save the village, the elders met and vowed to perform *The Passion Play*, which depicted the suffering, death, and resurrection of Jesus Christ, once every ten years. From that moment forward, it has been said that not another person died, though several had signs of the plague. The following year, *The Passion Play* was presented for the first time in fulfillment of the vow.

I saw Weiland walk in, and he waved to me. As he approached my table, I couldn't stop thinking about how beautiful he was. He was coming over to me; this was definitely a dream.

Weiland asked if he could join me for dinner. He asked if I were enjoying the town.

I told him I had gone shopping but I really did not see that much. I told him I had been thinking about going to *The Passion Play*, but it was canceled due to the war.

He kind of ignored what I said and asked if I would like to spend some time with him since he did not have any immediate plans.

I said I would love to and asked if he had anything in mind.

He suggested going to the mountains to do some sightseeing. I could not help but notice his incredibly beautiful eyes piercing through me. We agreed that tomorrow would be perfect.

He said we could get an early start at six o'clock.

At that moment, two men walked in. Weiland must have noticed them out of the corner of his eye because he swiftly took my hand and drew me closer. It looked like we were being intimate. He whispered in my ear, "Let me know when they are gone."

I had an eerie feeling while the men glanced around the room. I was happy when they left. I said, "That was strange, those men coming in here. They were definitely looking for someone." *What's going on?* I could ignore some things, but I was getting a little suspicious.

They had music playing softly in the background, and Weiland asked me to dance. I told him I didn't dance very well, and he said, "Don't worry. I'll lead."

When we got on the dance floor, he pulled me close. I could feel the chills go down my spine. He was tall and muscular, and I almost forgot about Kane.

After our dance, we sat down and started talking about where he was born. He opened up about his whole life, everything except what type of business he was in. He told me his business was very secretive, and once it was over, he would tell me everything. He told me not to worry, reassured me I was safe with him, and insisted he would never let anything happen to me.

Oddly, I trusted this man I had just met. I felt safe with him—like he could protect me no matter what. That felt good.

The evening was winding down, and I was ready to go to bed.

Weiland asked for my shoe size. When I told him that was personal, he said he needed to get me snow boots for tomorrow's outing.

"I promise I won't judge your foot size," he said.

When I told him, he looked at me with a little twinkle in his eye. He said, "I'll see you at six tomorrow morning."

When he left, I went into my room and drew a hot bubble bath. While I was in the bath, I thought about my day and how exciting it was to meet this mysterious man who totally intrigued me. I also thought about my dream on the island with Kane, and I hoped I would see him again.

Then my mind went to Weiland. I wondered how it would feel to make love to him. I got out of the tub and lay down. I had left the window open so I could see the mountains. I was finding it hard to fall asleep because I was thinking of Weiland. Finally, I fell asleep.

I awoke to someone knocking on the door, and I quickly put on my robe to see who was there. I looked through the peephole, and there was Weiland.

As I opened the door, he handed me the boots and asked if I was ready. It felt like I had slept for five minutes. I asked him to give me a minute to get ready. After I bundled up, we started for his jeep.

Weiland said we would drive as far as we could, but then we would have to hike the rest of the way. While driving toward the mountains, I thought I saw lights behind us. I did not say anything because they were gone when I looked again.

When we parked, Weiland came around to help me out. As I got out of the jeep, I slipped on some ice. As I fell into Weiland's arms, I thought I felt a gun on him. I did not say anything, but I wondered what I was getting myself into. I had to remind myself that it was a dream.

He held my hand as we walked toward the trail that led to the mountains. The weather was beautiful. The sun was rising up through the mountains. The air had a cool, crisp feel to it. The view of the mountains was breathtaking. The trail came to a suspended wooden footbridge. It did not look like it was made for people to walk over; it was narrow and had ropes as railings.

Weiland said, "This is where we are going to cross over. We have to be very careful. The ice on the bridge is very slippery, and we could easily fall."

He took my hand, and chills went down my spine. Once we got across safely, he turned toward me. Looking into my eyes, he kissed me. I felt a familiar feeling, like I had known him all my life, just like the feeling I had with Kane. There was such a strong connection between the two of us that I lost all thoughts of the island and Kane.

As Weiland held me, I could feel the gun. I had to ask why he was carrying a gun.

All of a sudden, we heard gunshots. He quickly pushed me behind some boulders. Weiland was shooting at the men. I could not believe what I was seeing. Everything was happening so fast. One of the men slipped on the bridge and fell through the ropes. The other ran off. An engine roared, and the rubber tires raced away.

Weiland came back as soon as he thought it was safe. I could not catch my breath; my heart was racing. He held me, rubbing my arms to calm me down. I told him he had to tell me what was going on. I was not going anywhere with him until he told me.

He said, "I'm so sorry. I did not mean for you to be in danger. Not here. I just wanted you to see the beauty of the mountains, and I wanted to be with you. I never wanted to put you in danger."

"Tell me what's going on."

He said, "I am a spy. My real name is Daniel. My friend, Jacob, was involved in a secret mission, which he didn't tell me about. Somehow his cover was revealed, and he had to go into hiding. He is in these mountains. For my protection, he still has not told me the type of mission he was involved in or about the people who are trying to track him down. He asked me to watch over his family. I've tried to keep them safe as he requested, but it is getting more and more dangerous for them. I fear he is in danger, and these men prove that I am right. These people want him dead, and they will do anything to make sure the job gets done. I have this strong feeling to be with you, though. I have never needed anyone before, and when my instincts are this strong, they are never wrong. I know better than to put someone in danger. I am so sorry."

"Don't do this. I want to be with you too," I said. "I feel the same way." I started to get cold, and Weiland—or Daniel—put his arms around me and held me tightly. Although I had only known him for such a short time, I'd never felt so safe in all my life. He exuded such confidence and strength that I could not help but be extremely attracted to him. I did not care if I could die. *I'd die with him,* I thought. *I have never met anyone so brave and so loyal.*

"I want to go with you," I said.

"It's too dangerous."

"I don't care. I just want to be with you."

CHAPTER 3

H e took my hand, and we began our journey up the mountain. Even though it was very cold, the sky was sunny and clear. We could see from the peaks of the mountaintops to the valleys below. The view was spectacular.

I was glad Daniel knew his way around the mountains because you could easily get lost. My snow boots kept my feet warm, and I was so grateful. I could not have endured the arduous hike without them. It was starting to get dark, and the temperature was starting to get even colder.

Daniel said we were going to rest for the night in a cave that was just ahead. I knew it sounded silly because of the journey we were on, but I asked if there were bats in the cave. I had a fear of bats.

He said, "I think we have more important things to worry about, don't you? But I'll protect you. Don't worry."

It was no surprise how prepared Daniel was when we got to the cave. He had everything we could possibly need in his backpack, including a blanket, some canned food, and an opener. Everything Daniel did was perfect and well thought out. I liked that about him. I did not have to worry about anything when I was with him. He took care of everything, which I loved.

After dinner, Daniel stretched out on the blanket and offered his arm to rest my head. I lay down beside him, and he just stared into my eyes as if he were trying to read my thoughts. I rested my head on his arm. He turned toward me and gently kissed my lips. I knew we were going to make love.

He slowly kissed me, touching me very gently. Somehow, without words, he made me feel like he never wanted anyone the way he wanted me. I always wanted a man to make me feel that way. I was enough, just me. My exhausted body was awakened like never before. He was very gentle as he kissed my lips and neck, moving so confidently all over my body. He was amazing in every way. I ached for him.

I could not wait for him to be inside of me. As he entered my body, he entered my soul. As we became one, I never imagined it could be so beautiful. When our bodies finally had enough, he held me like he would never let me go. I was convinced that he was made just for me.

When I woke in the morning, he was standing near the entrance of the cave and looking out. I said, "Good morning."

He looked at me with concern and said, "We have to go now. They are going to find us if we stay here any longer."

I quickly got myself together. As I went to grab Daniel's hand to leave, I woke up in my bed. It felt like I had been asleep for days. I stayed in bed for a while, trying to make sense of everything I had just been through. I had to get the kids up for school.

I got up, washed my face, and brushed my teeth. Finally, the pièce de résistance, my first cup of coffee made me so happy. I sat for a few minutes in peace before I woke up my lovely children for the day. Waking my kids up in the morning was special since it took about thirty minutes. I began by saying, "Wake up, sweetie," and I ended up screaming, "Wake up. We are going to be late!"

After I dropped them off at school, I had a few hours to myself. I took my time doing the laundry, cleaning, and running errands. It may not sound like it, but I was having a great day. I could not wait to go to bed and dream. I wondered what would happen that night.

My husband asked why I was in such a good mood.

I wanted to say, "Hey, I had the best sex of my life and found a man who made me feel like a woman!" I actually said, "I just had a great night's sleep, and I feel refreshed." It was the truth.

It was getting close to bedtime, and I could not wait. I washed the dishes in record time and prepared the kids' lunches for the following day so I could sleep a little longer in the morning. It was easy to get everything done with something to look forward to. I was so happy to rest my head on the pillow. My body melted into the bed, and I felt myself go into a deep sleep.

I woke up holding Daniel's hand. We started up the trail. It was colder than the day before. The sky was cloudy, and it looked like it was going to snow again. I could not imagine people doing this as a hobby.

The trail had a lot of ice and snow, which made a difficult hike even more laborious. As we were walking, I slipped on some ice.

Daniel tried to grab me before I went down the hill. If not for the trees, I would not have had anything to grab on to—and there was a cliff right below me. I was panicked, but I managed to keep myself steady until Daniel could get to me. I was losing my ability to hang on. I had used most of my energy during the hike. I was exhausted, and I was just about to give up.

When I had nothing left, Daniel appeared before me, holding his hand out to me. As I reached for him, I slipped. He threw himself at me, risking his own life. I could not believe this was happening; it was a dream, but it seemed so real.

Daniel had more in his backpack than I had realized. He had hoisted himself down with a rope and pulley to get to me. I was shaking and crying as he pulled me with all his might to him. He held me for what seemed to be the longest time.

Once I calmed down, we climbed back up to the trail. We found a safe place where we could rest for a bit.

Daniel told me how Jacob had once saved him when they were on a mission together. He said that Jacob could have left him, and anyone else would have.

"But he stayed with me, knowing he could die. He stayed with me even though he had a family and everything to live for. I will never forget that. I'm glad I could repay my friend," Daniel said.

We were getting closer. We started on the trail once again. Daniel was holding my hand very tightly. As we went around a huge bend, a helicopter headed in our direction. The people in the helicopter were shooting at us.

We ran toward some boulders. They were shooting at us in a way that created movement in the snow, and all of a sudden, the snow started to tumble toward us.

Daniel quickly grabbed hold of me, and we away from the oncoming snow. The helicopter was at our level, and the snow landed on the propeller and brought the helicopter down. We actually had to dive out of the way, escaping the avalanche only by inches. We held each other, and he once again assured me that he would protect me. We looked at each other, and it felt like a supreme oneness of love I had never experienced.

He said, "We should be meeting Jacob in about two hours. We will take him to meet with his wife and son."

Daniel promised me that we were safe. We climbed to the top of the mountain and back down the other side. We spotted a mother bear and her cubs, which was odd since they usually hibernated during that time of year. We saw a huge deer. He was standing in the open and looking at us. It was amazing to be so close to wildlife. It felt good to be with Daniel and holding his hand. I loved the intimacy of just being alone together and talking.

Daniel told me he felt that his connection with God deepened when he was in the mountains because everything is so pure and untouched.

We headed down the mountain. The wind was blowing. The sky was partly cloudy, and it was absolutely beautiful.

Daniel looked at me and said, "I never thought I'd be in this situation with such a beautiful woman." He held my hand even tighter.

I asked him how he got into this line of work.

He said he had a hard childhood due to the war, and he saw a lot of people die. He had watched his own brother get shot and killed. He said, "I swore to myself that I would do my part to make this world a safer place."

As we came down the mountain, we crossed over the border into the most beautiful area I had ever seen. The openness of the hills reminded me of *The Sound of Music*. It was probably the same area. I asked Daniel where we were, but he didn't answer.

As we approached the cabin where Jacob had been hiding, we saw smoke in the sky. We were headed toward a dense forest. We were just about to knock on the cabin door when Jacob opened it very quickly. He was covered in animal fur and was pointing a gun at us. Once he realized it was Daniel, they embraced like brothers who had not seen each other in years.

When Daniel introduced me, Jacob looked puzzled.

Daniel said, "I will explain later."

It was a small, open cabin. There were no walls to separate the rooms, and the bathroom was outside. It had a small loft with a bed that was on the floor. The bed was stuffed with hay, and it was covered with animal fur, which had the worst stench. It took some time to get used to the odor. I had never actually been in a cabin like this one. It reminded me of *Little House on the Prairie*. It was hard to imagine that people lived like that.

Jacob had a wood-burning stove, and water had to be brought in from outside. It was rough living, that's for sure. Jacob was so excited that we were there, and he wanted to celebrate with food and wine.

Daniel had some food left from the night before, and Jacob had been saving a bottle of wine. We had the most enjoyable dinner. Daniel didn't waste any time. He told Jacob he had passports; everything was arranged for us to leave first thing in the morning.

The wine went right to my head. I had to go to bed. Daniel helped me get up to the loft and sat me down on the bed, which was warm and comfortable. The animal skin was so thick that the hay could not poke through. I was happy to lie down; it had been an exhausting journey.

Daniel made sure I was comfortable before going downstairs to talk to Jacob. The wine made me very sleepy. When I woke up, Daniel was holding me. I wished that we were alone. I wanted him to make love to me just like in the cave.

Daniel wrapped his strong arms around me. How could I feel anything but love? No words were necessary to feel the love we had toward each other. I dozed off, wondering what the next day would hold for us.

I woke up in my bed with the sunlight shining through the window. I was disappointed that I was not with Daniel. I knew I had to get my day going. I quickly got up, got my husband off to work, and got the kids up and ready for school. I had a ten o'clock hair appointment, and I rushed to get some things done first.

I arrived a few minutes early, hoping to get in sooner than my scheduled appointment. I ran into my girlfriend who had just gone through a divorce; she was getting her hair done too. We started talking about our families and what was going on in our lives.

She told me about a dream that was like a fairytale. Her true love had come and swept her away, and she felt an undeniable love that she had never experienced before. She said she hated to wake up.

To me, the dream symbolized what my girlfriend wanted most in her life. I didn't bother going into my dreams. It was complicated.

I was preparing dinner at home when my husband came into the kitchen and told me that we were celebrating the settlement of a big case he had been working on for quite some time. I was happy for him, but it was hard to get close to him and feel excited after being with Daniel. Even though it was a dream, it felt very different for me.

That night, I went to bed—and I woke up with Daniel. I was so happy to be back with him. I could smell bacon cooking. I could even hear the crackling of the bacon in the black cast iron skillet. I love the aroma of bacon. It reminded me of when I was a young child and my dad made a big Sunday breakfast. Jacob had just caught a wild boar before we arrived. Much to my surprise, the bacon was delicious. I'm not big on the taste of gamey meats, but it was very good. Jacob also made some fresh bread for breakfast.

After Jacob buried the remains of the wild boar and disposed of all traces of anyone staying in the cabin, we were off. As we started down the mountain, I noticed we were headed in a completely different direction.

Jacob led the way. Daniel and I were right behind, holding hands. I didn't know what was going to happen when we got to the train station, and I didn't want to ask. I knew what would happen, but I was with Daniel, which was all I wanted to know.

We came upon a patch of ice, and Daniel jokingly said, "No more slipping for you." He carefully guided me across.

We could see the small town ahead. It was not as far as I thought it would be. I could feel my heart breaking already because I knew what would happen once we met up with Jacob's family.

The train station was small. It was nothing like the train station in Oberammergau. It was much more rustic, like a small town from an old western movie. I kept waiting to see tumbleweeds float by.

There was a small cabin to the right of the station. Daniel said that was where Jacob's family was staying.

A petite, beautiful woman ran out toward Jacob. They grabbed each other for a long time, sobbing. She turned to Daniel and thanked him for bringing Jacob safely back to them. His son came out behind his mother, crying. The whole scene was very emotional.

I looked at Daniel, and tears ran down his face. After everyone regained their composure, Daniel introduced me to Jacob's family. We all went to the cabin where Jacob's wife had cooked turkey, mashed potatoes, vegetables, stuffing, and homemade popovers. It was a feast. It was perfect to have a home-cooked meal after our journey.

Daniel told everyone that the train was leaving at four o'clock, and they had to be on it. He had all the paperwork, and everything was set.

Jacob was impressed with how thorough Daniel was with all the planning. As it got close to four, I had to ask the dreaded question. I said, "Are you leaving too?"

He said, "I have to go with them. We still have some unfinished business, but I've arranged for a car to take you back to the hotel."

"Will I ever see you again?" I asked.

"Yes, we will meet again."

We held each other for the longest time.

He said, "Till we meet again." Those were his last words to me.

As I watched the train leave, I got into the car. It was a long, lonely ride back to the hotel.

He's not here, I told myself. I got to my room and went right to bed.

I woke up with the sun shining through my bedroom window. I realized that I was home. I had overslept and rushed to get my husband and kids up and out of the house.

While I was rushing around doing my daily errands, I could not help but wonder where I would be tonight.

CHAPTER 4

ↀ

Ifinally got home after running around all day, and while
I was getting dinner ready, the doorbell rang. I opened
the door, and a deliveryman held an incredible bouquet of
sunflowers. I quickly read the card to see who they were from. It
read: "To Rayne, I love you. Michael."

My husband had sent them. I wondered what the occasion
was. *What is today's date? Is it our anniversary?* When he got home,
I asked him what the occasion was.

He simply said, "You had a horrible night's sleep. You were
tossing and turning, so I thought flowers would lift your spirits."

I gave him a big hug, and we had a very nice evening together,
just relaxing and watching television. It was almost time for bed,
and I wondered where in the world I would wake up. I fell asleep,
and the next thing I knew, I was on my back. I noticed right off
that something was not right. I did not feel right. I stretched my
arm over my head, and it splashed into water.

I looked around, and I was surrounded by water. I was drifting
on a piece of wood. I looked in the distance and saw a ship on fire.
It was sinking. I had such an eerie feeling seeing the ship go down.
Ever since I was a young girl, I had a fear of sinking boats. I went

to move my hair from my eyes to make sure I was seeing properly. I discovered blood all over my hand. My head was bleeding.

I was trying to think clearly, but it was difficult. I knew I was drifting on wood. I had a wound on my head, and I was wearing a white cotton dress. All of a sudden, I heard the swishing of water. When I turned to look, I saw a rowboat coming right at me. There was a huge man in the front of the boat. He looked like a pirate. I was trying to make sense of what I was seeing. Had I gone to bed watching *Pirates of the Caribbean*? Was Captain Jack Sparrow coming to get me? *I wish!*

I said, "Where am I?"

He was very gentle and took great concern as he lifted me into the boat. I must have passed out because I woke up on a huge bed with a red velvet bedspread and silk sheets; candles lit the room. I was wondering how in the world I had gotten there. I remembered drifting on the water, and the man with the funny hat lifting me.

The cabin door opened, and the captain walked in the room. He was very charismatic. He was surprised that I was awake. He had a cloth in his hand. As he approached me, I could not help but notice his deep, dark, beautiful eyes looking at me with such care. He said, "I'm just going to check your head. You have a pretty deep gash. Do you know what happened?"

I just looked at him like a frightened puppy.

He said, "Your boat was filled with women and young girls who were going to be sold as slaves. We sank the ship and tried to save as many as we could, including you."

I must have looked horrified because he quickly assured me that he was not going to hurt me. He put the cloth on my head and said, "This is my cabin. I thought you would be safer in here. I'm Captain John Taylor."

How in the world did I get here? What kind of dream is this? I could not figure out how I hit my head. Fragments of memory started to flash through my mind. The Captain on the slave ship wanted to keep me for his own pleasure. I tried to get away, but he came after me in a very violent manner. He was trying to intimidate me by hitting me. I remember his breath had a very strong odor of old rum as he was ripping my dress off. That explains the white cotton underdress I was wearing. I was trying to get away when the sound of a loud cannon went off. At that same moment, he hit me in the head with a gun. I lost consciousness. I tried desperately to get my thoughts together. *What is going to happen to me?*

We heard a knock at the cabin door.

The captain said, "Come in." He turned to me and said, "I thought you might be hungry. I had dinner prepared for us." The sterling silver, fine china, gorgeous wine goblets, beautiful red velvet chairs, and mahogany table were very impressive. He had impeccable taste. Everything was perfect, just like him. *Maybe he is a pirate so he can have these beautiful belongings.*

The smell of the food was making me hungry. He helped me over to the table. I could not believe how weak I was. I wondered what kind of person John Taylor was—ruthless like the captain on the slave ship or a captain who had a heart?

As we sat down to eat, he put his legs up on the table, crossing them. He leaned back in his chair, holding his wine goblet. He was very comfortable with himself, cocky and conceited. He knew he was handsome and smart. As I was eating, he stared at me. He said, "You are so beautiful. You have an air of royalty. I can't figure out what it is about you."

I said, "I don't remember anything. I've been trying to gather my thoughts, but my mind is blank."

"It'll take a few days to get your memory back. In the meantime, this cabin is yours. During your time on the ship, I will stay on the upper deck."

I could not help but wonder why he was being so nice to me. I said, "I don't have clothes."

He said, "You are welcome to whatever you can find in this room. If you prefer, we have dresses down below."

"No, thank you," I said. "Besides, I would be uncomfortable in a gown."

He excused himself for the evening. I was happy to be alone. I absorbed everything that was happening. I rummaged through some drawers and found a pair of black pants. I checked to see if they had an odor, but they did not. I got a knife from the table and cut them into shorts. I found a white silk shirt and a big black belt. I belted the shirt like a pirate. It was not the look I was going for, but it worked out that way. I was comfortable.

I gazed out the porthole and wondered where I'd come from. I was lost. I wished my memory would come back, but it was like a fog. When my head started throbbing, I went to sleep.

I awoke to the smell of coffee and bacon. Captain John's arrogance amused me. Maybe it would have been annoying if he were obnoxious, but he was so charming that he could get away with doing what he wanted. He knew how to polish his rough edges. He had a certain quality that was very appealing and sexy. He said, "You look like a pirate."

I said, "Thank you. Can I go up on deck?"

He said, "Yes, of course. There are some girls up there."

As I approached the door, he grabbed me and kissed me. I pulled away, not knowing what would come next. "Why did you do that?" I asked.

He said, "I am very attracted to you. Yes, you are beautiful, but it's more than your beauty. I'm drawn to you. I had to kiss you. I have to admit the kiss almost brought me to my knees."

He escorted me to the upper deck. Much to my surprise, the pirates were very respectful, tilting their hats as I walked by. They were totally unlike the savages on the other ship who were out to steal and take advantage of people. The pirates on this ship were like the good-hearted captain.

I saw some of the girls at the far end of the ship. I wanted to talk to them to see if they had any information about where I came from. I could feel the captain watching every move I made. It was not a weird feeling. It was comforting, like he was being protective. I could feel him with every ounce of my being, and I liked it.

One of the girls said, "You're the one they took off a private ship while it was docked. Your family had gone into town, and you were waving at them from the deck. The captain noticed you right away, and what he wanted, he took. He claimed you as his property. Your crew tried to protect you. Even at the risk of their own lives, they were fighting with the pirates until their deaths. When the fighting was over, they threw you into a big burlap bag to get control over you, and that's all I know."

Captain John walked up behind me, listening intently to what the girl had to say.

With tears in her eyes, she thanked him again. "I remember all the girls talking about how beautiful your dress was. It was made with the finest silks. I wish I could tell you more because I know what it's like to be taken from your family. I was taken from mine. I was shopping in town with my sister when they took me. I'm so grateful to Captain John Taylor because I know some girls who have been sold into slavery and never heard from again."

The other girls were younger, and I don't think they understood what would have happened to them if they were not saved.

The water was so peaceful, and the pirates sang an old pirate song. It was actually very nice. They were happy and cheerful. It was comforting to being with them. It was like being home.

The captain said, "It won't be long before we get to the nearest port. We'll let you off to find your families."

He looked at me with longing in his eyes; I felt as if he wanted me to stay. He told us that he and the crew would like to have a celebratory dinner with dancing that evening. He looked at me and said, "I hope you will come."

I said, "Yes, I would love to."

He went up to his first mate, the gentleman steering the ship, and took over.

I walked up so I could be beside him. While I was standing there, he asked if I would like to steer. He put me in front of the helm and stood behind me. I could feel his body up against mine as he put his arms around mine, guiding my hands as I steered the ship.

I asked him why he was a pirate. He did not seem like the typical pirate type.

He said, "I had two sisters who were sold into slavery. Ever since then, I've been on a mission to save as many girls as I can since I was not able to save my sisters. Do you want to be a pirate? You have the outfit, and now you are steering the ship."

I could tell he wanted to change the subject. I could feel his heart breaking. The wind started to pick up, and my hair was blowing all over. I asked for a hat to control my hair.

He laughed arrogantly and said, "You can have one of mine."

The wind was picking up, and he called for someone to steer the ship. He took me back to the cabin. I loved the attention he was giving me. He made me feel special, and he was very respectful too.

When we got to the cabin, there was a beautiful gown on the bed. He said, "You might want to wear this tonight."

I said, "I like what I have on."

"You can put that back on tomorrow." He pulled me close to him, but he didn't kiss me. He said, "I want you to know that I'm not like the other pirates."

I was hoping he would kiss me.

He said, "I'll see you tonight for dinner."

When he left, I felt a rush of joy and threw myself on to the bed. I was thinking about how handsome he was. I stared at the ceiling and lost myself in thought. *What kind of man is he? Is he someone I can trust?* It would be a relief to let my guard down and absolutely trust him without having to worry about any ulterior motives.

I needed some time to see the true person that he was, but there was no way he could be fake. My mind kept going back and forth with these thoughts until I dozed off.

I woke up to a soft knock at the door. One of the girls asked if I was ready. I told her I would meet her at the party. I started to fix my hair. It was pretty messy from the wind.

He said I could help myself to anything in his room. In a chest, I found a beautiful clustered pearl hair comb, and I put it in my hair. I have to admit it looked very pretty. I put the gown on, and it was a bit tight. Although the dress looked more appropriate, I felt more comfortable with my shorts and white shirt. I changed back into my comfortable clothes.

What is it about these clothes that I like so much? I felt really good. It suited the way I was feeling, and off I went.

I heard music coming from the dining hall, and when I opened the door, everyone stopped to look at me.

Captain John asked me where my gown was.

I said, "Thank you, but I prefer what I have on."

He laughed and escorted me to his table.

I was not surprised to see a feast fit for a king and his court on the table. They had wine by the barrels, and it was delicious. The music was playing, and everyone was dancing.

He asked if I would like to dance. I never imagined pirates slow dancing, but they do. We looked into each other's eyes, and it seemed as if we were one soul. I had never had that experience. We were one. We were lost in each other. It went through my whole body.

He held me close. I think he felt me trembling. He whispered, "I can't resist you."

I could not believe how powerful the feeling was, and I needed to pull myself together.

We went to the upper deck to get some fresh air. He put his arms around me. I did not want him to let me go. I do not think he wanted to let me go either.

He said, "I don't know what I'm feeling. I've never felt like this before."

I could not believe how open he was with his emotions. He spoke very honestly. All I wanted was to be with him. I wished the moment could last forever. I felt so complete with him.

I asked him to teach me how to be a pirate. If he could teach me how to take care of myself, then maybe I could help save the other girls who were captured.

He grabbed my hand and asked, "Do you think you could do what I do and fight pirates? Do you think you could handle a sword?"

For some reason, I felt I could. I looked at him and said, "I think I could if you teach me."

He let go of my hand and started to walk away. He turned and threw the sword at me; surprisingly, I caught it like a master swordsman.

"How did you do that?" he asked.

I said, "I don't know."

He responded, "Hopefully you will get your memory back soon."

The wine made me sleepy, and we headed back to the captain's quarters.

I told him I felt guilty for taking his bed.

He said, "I don't mind the hammock."

"Have you slept on the hammock before?"

"No, I've never slept on the hammock until now. I've never given my bed to anyone until now." He held my hand the whole way.

I enjoyed being close to him. I wanted him, and the wine made me want him even more. I looked at him and asked, "Do you want to sleep on the couch?"

Without saying anything, he lifted me up and swung me around the room, kissing me as we fell onto his bed. He was the most intimate, gentle man I had ever met. The love he gave to me was unbelievable and electrifying. I never thought making love could be so beautiful. He caressed my arms and held my face as he kissed me. He looked into my eyes and truly saw me.

He was patient and thoughtful. His pleasure was giving me pleasure, watching me, giving to me sexually, spiritually, and emotionally. He gave the kind of love everyone wanted but rarely received.

After we made love, we fell asleep in each other's arms. I woke up and noticed that the porthole was open. I could feel the water coming in from the waves hitting the ship. I looked around the cabin, but he wasn't there.

I got up and dressed. My clothes smelled and needed to be washed. I put on the dress from the night before and went to the upper deck.

He was at the helm.

I asked him why he had not woken me up.

He said, "You looked so peaceful. I didn't want to disturb you. Are you ready to be a pirate?

"Yes, I'm ready."

He said, "Good. After breakfast, we will begin your lesson."

Why am I doing this? Why am I so willing to use a sword and learn how to be a pirate? Why? Who am I?

After breakfast, we got started. He threw me the sword again, and I caught it. He put his hand behind him like he was in a swordfight, and I took the position of a swordsman. Before anything further could happen, I woke up in my bed. *Why did my dream cut off?* I did not know what was going on. I got up and got my kids ready for school.

It was a particularly fun morning. Everyone was laughing and joking with each other. I could not help but wonder what I was missing in my life. Something was missing, but what? I could not wait to go to bed. I did my usual routine.

After dinner, I did the dishes and got everything ready for the morning. I kissed my husband and told him I was going to bed. *I have a man who loves me, and I have wonderful children. What more do I want? Why have my dreams been my outlet? Are they giving me something I am desperately seeking? What do my dreams mean? I crave excitement. I crave an exciting love! That is what I am missing. I do not know where I will end up, but I hope I go back to where I left off.*

My hopes came true, and my dream came alive. I was holding a sword.

Captain John asked, "Are you sure you have never held a sword?"

I said, "I told you I don't remember anything."

He assured me that my memory would return. It might take some time, but it would return. We would be at port soon, and everyone would be free to go.

He looked at me, and his mouth was moving. He was speaking, but I could not believe what I was hearing. He said, "You are free to go."

I was anything but free. I did not know what had come over me. My mind and body were overwhelmed by emotion. He could see in my eyes that I was staying. No words were necessary. He took me into his arms and asked, "Are you sure?"

I replied, "I know that I want to be by your side so we can fight this war together."

He looked at me with the most loving eyes. That night, as I was standing on the main deck and looking at the moonlit ocean, it looked so peaceful. I felt someone come up behind me. He put his hand on my shoulder, and I immediately felt the passion between us ignite. He kissed me with such a deep and sincere love that I knew there was no place else I wanted to be but with him.

When he was done, he said, "I hope you don't mind. I could not resist."

A smiling crewman walked by and tipped his hat as he passed. Although we were in the midst of such evil, the captain and the crewmen were the most respectful group of men. They made all the women and girls feel very safe.

We sat on the steps and talked about his brothers and sisters. His older brother was killed trying to protect his sisters. He and his twin brother were so young at the time and didn't know what to do. He was never able to forgive himself, and he vowed to do whatever it took to find his sisters and save others from this horror. A friend taught him how to use a sword, and he eventually became an extremely skilled swordsman. He said, "That man was like a father to me. He taught me everything I know. When he died, he left me this ship. I've been on a mission ever since. I've been looking for my sisters and saving as many girls and women as I can. I don't know if my sisters are still alive, but I will never give up."

He had such a beautiful heart. It was easy to open up to him. I was starting to get chilly.

He said, "Let me walk you to your cabin. Do you remember anything?"

I said, "Not yet."

He said, "That bump on your head doesn't help."

As we got to the cabin, I said, "Don't go. Stay with me."

He helped me get undressed, kissed my back, and unbuttoned my dress. He caressed my shoulders gently. He was sweet and strong. He could have been a monster, but he was anything but that. I had to gather my senses and think about how tenderly he treated me. I craved him. My body was engulfed in a raging heat of passion.

I turned around and pulled him down on top of me. As we kissed, I could feel the fire flow through our bodies. When we were too exhausted to give anything else, we fell asleep. I did not want to fall asleep. I did not want to leave him. I strained to keep myself awake.

I must have fallen asleep because I woke up to my children screaming.

"He took my cell phone!"

"She broke mine!"

On and on it went. *It is going to be a lovely day. The kids do not have school today. That is why they were up.*

We decided to go to the zoo and have lunch with my husband. I could not stop thinking about my dream and the passion I felt with Captain John. *What is going to happen in my real life? Am I missing so much love that I have to dream about it? I really need to figure out what I am missing.*

That night, my husband wanted to be passionate. I went along with it because that was what a good wife does. My husband was very different from Kane, Daniel, or Captain John Taylor. There was no romance with my husband. Maybe I had created these men because I needed that type of love in my life. I went to sleep while thinking about my marriage, my dreams, and what it all meant.

I woke up on the ship. I got up and looked out of the porthole. It looked like a beautiful, sunny day. I got dressed and went to the main deck. I was standing near the side of the boat, and Captain John walked up to me with a cup of coffee. The thrill of seeing him excited me. I could feel my body go weak just at the sight of him.

"Today we are going to go through a few simple lessons with the sword to see how you do. The other day might have been a little bit of beginner's luck," he said.

Much to everyone's surprise, I had some hidden talent. I handled the sword with skill and confidence. I felt as though I had been born with a sword in my hand. It was very natural for me. I saw a rope above me, and I hit it with my sword.

All of a sudden, one of the crewmen yelled, "Ship on the harbor bound."

The air immediately changed from jolly laughter to silence. Instantly, it was clear to me why John was the captain. He took control and planned out the strategy brilliantly. I was very impressed with his leadership and authority. He told me to go down below.

I said, "No. I want to be part of this. I told you that."

He was taken aback that I didn't obey his command.

Everything happened fast. The cannons blasted, the swords came out, and all hell broke loose. Once we had control of their ship, there was only one rule: the captain and crew were killed.

When it was safe to board the ship, the captain, some crewmen, and I got into a rowboat to rescue the girls. We went down below, searching for the rest of the girls. We found them gathered like cattle in a room.

Captain Taylor introduced himself and said, "We aren't going to harm you. We are here to rescue you."

They had me go over to comfort the girls. While I got the girls together, the captain and his crew became the pirates they loathed. They took all the food and liquor and anything worth any value. It was not a surprise that the girls came from every walk of life. There was no preference for what type of woman or girl had been captured.

When they were done pillaging, they sank the ship. It was haunting to see a ship that was once bigger than life sink.

That evening, I was happy to hear music coming from the dining hall. The girls were talking and laughing, and the crewmen were singing. The captain was sitting on a barrel of wine. When he spotted me, he got up to greet me. We went up to the main deck to hear each other better. I looked out at the ocean. *Maybe this type of life is for me. Maybe this is what I'm meant to do.*

Suddenly, I felt the warmth of his hand on my shoulder. He turned me around and kissed me, but this kiss was different. It was as if we were one, like our souls belonged to one another. I knew it was a moment I would never forget. Moments were all we had to hold on to. I wanted to hold on to that one.

He looked at me and smiled. I could tell he felt the same way. He said, "You surprised me today. You really handled it well. Maybe you were brought up to be a pirate. Do you have any memory at all?"

I said, "No. Not yet."

We began walking the ship, and we ended up at the cabin.

He said, "Tomorrow we head for port to let the girls go. There will be another trip. Are you sure you want to stay on with us?"

"I told you once, and I'll say it again: I'm staying."

As we approached the cabin and opened the door, I said, "I don't want to be alone tonight. Will you stay?"

He lifted me up and brought me over to the bed, kissing me and holding me like he would never let me go. In his arms, I thought about my life and what I wanted. It opened my mind to the possibilities of a lot of things, and I knew I wanted him to be a part of my life.

I thought he was asleep when I heard him say, "It's going to be a rough week. There is an African warlord, and he's taking black women and white women. He has a vicious reputation. I don't know if I want you on board for this fight."

"As long as I'm beside you, I have no fear."

And then I woke up in my bed. The children had school, but they were fast asleep and waiting for me to wake them. They were so good—not!

I said, "Wake up, my little sweets." And I ended up yelling, "Wake up!" Oh, the start of another beautiful morning.

Everyone started the day, and I was alone at last. I had no plans. I took some time to think about my life and what I really needed to be happy. The first thing that came to mind was love. I also came to the realization that I was afraid of facing my fears. Why was love popping into my mind? I had love. I had a wonderful husband. What was I thinking? Maybe I did not have the love I needed, the kind of love that filled my heart and my soul the way I needed or wanted it to.

Why was facing my fears popping up in my mind? I knew what it was. It was the fear of confronting my husband and the fear of losing my family, my home, and the security of what my husband and I had built together. I was going to have to talk to him, but he was so busy. What would I say? I had to make sense. I couldn't just talk nonsense. This was important. This issue would either bring us closer and open the door to a better understanding of each other or end our marriage. Was there no love? What could I say? "Honey, I've been having these dreams, but they are not only dreams. I have been so lonely and so unhappy. I have been thinking that our relationship is missing a deep intimacy, which is a very important component that I need to truly be happy." No, I could not say that. I would have to think about what I really needed to say to him. I wanted to be clear about my feelings.

As I fell asleep that night, the words "the truth will set you free" kept going through my mind. I was afraid of the truth because I knew the truth would change my life completely.

I woke up on the main deck, waiting for the captain. While looking at the water, I noticed a fin circling. As I looked closer, I realized it was huge shark. I thought it was feeding on something, but I could not see what it was. My mind started thinking about how free the shark seemed and how peaceful it was gliding through the water. It was not responsible for anything but itself, roaming wherever the current went at that moment. I could not help but think how nice it would be to really be free. The captain came up behind me and put his hand on my shoulder. It was strange how peaceful he made me feel with one touch of his hand. I really trusted him. He had a concerned look as I turned to look at him.

I said, "The sea looks so beautiful and calm."

He said, "Not for long. Captain Black is headed this way. We are going to sail around this area until we meet up with his ship."

We headed toward the helm because he wanted to check with his crewmen to see if everything was ready for the upcoming battle. It was amazing how in control he was, knowing that death could be right around the corner for us. He was very easy to talk to and did not keep anything hidden. He shared his thoughts and feelings about everything.

He sat down and put his legs up just like the first night I met him. He had a very comfortable way about him. I was completely attracted to him. He told me that I intrigued him because I had a lot of spirit and a whole lot of love to give.

"I just want to know who I am," I said.

We spoke about what we wanted in life. We talked about our personal dreams of family and children, and we agreed that we liked the excitement of helping people and freeing the women who had been enslaved.

It was dusk, and the crewmen were singing old pirate songs while cleaning the ship and mopping the deck. The captain and I went back to his quarters to be alone. We somehow knew it would be our most memorable night together. Not knowing what was to come tomorrow, he was especially gentle and pleasing in every way.

At dawn, we heard the crewmen yelling, "Ship coming."

A horrible feeling came over me as we quickly got dressed. We went up to the main deck, and the captain looked through the telescope at Captain Black's ship. He told his men to get prepared.

I looked at him and said, "What should I do?"

He said, "You stand by my side."

I woke to the smell of coffee. My husband had brought me a nice hot cup of coffee. *I love waking up to coffee in bed.* I sipped my coffee and thought about my dream. The word *freedom* came to my mind. I tried to think about what that meant to me. *I like being married. I like being in a committed relationship.* So what was it about freedom that was on my mind? *I have to get up and start my day. I will have to think about what is going on with my dreams later.*

During the course of the day, I could not help but think of freedom and what that meant in my life. My dreams were definitely telling me about something I needed to face in my life. *Why is it so hard for me to face myself?* I always prided myself on being able to look at my shortcomings when trying to improve or fix something about myself. *Why is this so different?*

I knew I was afraid, but knowing was not good enough anymore. I had to face this come what may. I knew it was happening to me because of my choices in life. They were not the best. I had chosen to bury my true self and hide who I really was, but it was all coming back to me. I had nowhere to turn. I would die if I did not face what scared me the most because the unhappiness was unbearable. I thought I was strong enough to handle what had happened to me years earlier. I thought time could heal all wounds. I thought creating a new life would be the answer to my regrets.

I could not wait to get back to the captain. I went to bed early and hoped I would get back to him. I was watching from the main deck as the crewmen took directions from the captain. All the men were getting ready, preparing and loading the cannons, and sharpening their swords.

The captain looked gorgeous as he held his sword. The wind was blowing his hair. He looked so strong and confident. He was everything I had ever wanted in a man. He was my friend, and we talked so easily about anything. He was a wonderful lover. He was reliable and caring, and he had the most beautiful heart. He was amazing in every way.

I walked over to a sword on the deck and picked it up. I started to play with it. I tried it out to see how it felt. It felt like I was born with a sword in my hand. I looked over, and the captain was staring at me.

He said, "You really look gorgeous."

I said, "I remember who I am. My dad is the greatest swordsman in all of Europe, LaGapel. He taught me everything I know about sword fighting."

With great surprise in his voice, he said, "You are LaGapel's daughter?"

We heard a cannon go off. The ship was getting closer. We could see the girls on the main deck. They must have thought that would deter Captain John and his crew from fighting.

Captain John warned me to stay away from the fighting. He said, "I'll watch out for you."

Without hesitation, the men said, "We'll watch out for her too."

Before I knew it, the fight had begun. The swords were swinging, the cannons were going off, and there was havoc everywhere. I lost track of my captain. I was frantically looking everywhere for him. I saw an ugly big man. From the description, it had to be Captain Black. I wanted to get a better look at who he was fighting with, and then I noticed it was John. My heart started racing. I saw him swing down the ropes to where I was.

He was protecting me from a pirate who was about to stab me with his sword. John was concerned with me, and he turned his back to help me.

Captain Black stabbed John.

I woke up in my bed. I couldn't believe I had woken up. I had to get back to John. He needed me. *Okay, this is just a dream. Get yourself together. I really need a reality check.*

I decided to get my day going and forget about my dream for the moment. I knew it sounded funny, but I couldn't bear to lose Captain John. I had never met someone who captivated me the way he did. Captain John was everything I ever wanted in a man. I could not believe myself. Was I that delusional that I had allowed myself to get caught up in a dream as if it were real? As if Captain John were real?

Get yourself together. I definitely need a Rayne check.

I called a friend to have lunch. I got through the rest of the day, picked up the kids, and made dinner. I could not wait to fall asleep, but I was too anxious. I got out of bed and made some hot chocolate to calm me down. Soon after that, I did fall asleep.

When I woke up, Captain John was looking at me with the most loving eyes. I knew it was not good because he was in a puddle of blood. I was so engrossed that I did not realize I had an audience.

"You are now mine, wench," Captain Black said. "I'm taking you with me."

I'm going to kill you. You have just destroyed my whole life.

We started to sword fight. Although he was much bigger, I was light on my feet. It was easy to tire him out. My dad must have taught me that strategy.

Everyone around me was fighting too. I noticed that John was still alive, and he was looking at me. I finally got the revenge I wanted. There was a small window, and I stabbed Captain Black in the heart. I thought it would feel different to kill him, but it did not. I felt empty and numb inside.

I ran over to John, held him in my arms, and told him I loved him. He could not speak, but I knew by looking in his eyes that he loved me too. I told him I would take over where he left off. I held him for what seemed to be an eternity.

I did not realize the fighting had stopped. When I looked up, everybody was staring at us.

Captain Black's crew had stopped too. Their evil leader had died, and they were released. Silence echoed through the ship.

Captain John's crewmen told me they had orders to put me in command if anything happened to him.

I said, "Me, captain? Why?"

I leaped up with a surge of empowerment. I raised my sword and proclaimed freedom for all women who had been enslaved.

The crewmen cheered! As they cheered, I knew I would do anything in my power to bring John's dreams to reality. The men wrapped his body and prepared him for a traditional burial. When they lowered his body into the ocean, I could feel my heart go with him.

CHAPTER 5

❦

I *am a woman of my word. I will keep my promise to John.* As this thought was going through my mind, I woke up in my bed. *How can I keep my promise if it was just a dream?* The thought saddened me.

I had to get my real day going. It was hard for me to shake the sadness. I truly felt as though I had lost someone I deeply loved. That aching feeling in my heart reminded me of when my father died. I seriously needed to think about something else. Helping my daughter with her homework, listening to her practice singing, and watching my son play basketball got my mind off my dream.

After dinner, I sat on the porch with a cup of tea. The mist in the air reminded me of the misty sea air on the ship with Captain John. I was getting sleepy, and I went to bed. I wondered where my dreams would take me. Lo and behold, I was back on the ship in John's quarters. *What is going on? Am I really back here?*

I heard tapping on the door, and I thought it could be John. Instead, it was Andre, John's best friend—the one person John completely trusted.

He said, "Good morning. Would you like some coffee? John told me you liked coffee first thing in the morning."

Andre was definitely a welcoming sight, and the coffee was a bonus.

I thanked him.

He said, "John told me to look after you, and that is what I am going to do, Bell."

As he was leaving, I asked him to come back later so we could talk. He had a puzzled look on his face. I thought Andre could help me keep my promise to John by helping me find John's sisters.

After he left, I stayed in the cabin all morning. When I finally got up, I put together an outfit from John's old clothes. *I am here, and I'm going to be who I said I would be.* It felt good to take control.

Andre knocked on the door and said, "Bell, what do you want to know? How can I help you?" Andre was older and very wise.

I said, "I need you to tell me about John and his sisters."

"I will tell you," he said. "I wanted to help him, and now I will help you. Did John tell you that he had a twin brother?"

"No," I said.

"He did not want to help John go after their sisters. John left him and his mother behind and never returned. The only way John was going to return was with his two sisters. Let's start by going to John's home once we dock."

Going to John's home seemed like a good place to start our journey. I was lonely being in John's cabin and knowing he was not going to walk through the door. I fell asleep for a bit.

Someone yelled, "Land ho."

We had arrived in port. I did not get off the ship right away. I wrote a note to my family to let them know I was okay.

Andre waited to take me to John's home. It was dusk by the time we got on our way. On the main street, drunks were having a good time hooting and hollering in the bars.

We finally arrived at John's house and knocked on the door.

A gentleman opened the door, and I knew immediately it was John's twin. He said, "Can I help you?"

I introduced us.

He said, "I'm Christopher."

We told him what had happened to John and about our intentions to find his sisters since it was John's last wish.

"I saw your ship come in this afternoon. I was hoping it was my brother. I do not want my mother to know about John. It's best if she does not know. It could kill her. I will meet you on the ship later tonight."

Andre and I went back to the ship to wait for Christopher. When we got back, I was in need of something strong. I asked Andre to join me for a shot of whiskey. I think we both felt like we had seen a ghost.

"Andre," I said, "I knew they were twins, but I did not expect to see an identical person."

After he left, I fell asleep while I waited for Christopher to arrive.

I woke up in my bed. The sun was shining through my blinds. So many thoughts were running through my mind. I wondered if I would go back that night.

The day went by fast. I could not wait to go to bed and return to the ship. I was happy to wake up in John's room.

Andre tapped on the door and said, "Are you up?"

"Sure, come on in. Stay and have some coffee with me, Andre. We have to get started. I don't think Christopher is going to show up."

"All right," he said. "Let's get on our way. I'll meet you on the upper deck. In the meantime, I will get the ship ready to sail."

I got dressed and went to the main deck.

Andre was giving the crew orders. He explained our mission to them and our promise to Captain John. Everyone was eager to assist.

As we were getting ready to set sail, Christopher said, "Can I come?"

Andre and I looked at each other and asked him what had changed his mind.

He said, "I let my brother down once, and I do not want to let him down again. Besides, I have a couple of sisters out there. I have to be honest with you. I am not a fighter. I do not know the first thing about sword fighting. I do not even know how to hold a sword!"

I said, "You can be a part of the crew. I will teach you how to use a sword. If you are willing to follow directions, you can come with us."

He looked at me.

Andre and the rest of the crew rubbed their heads and said, "I'm on board."

I told Andre to find him a bed.

Christopher looked at me with a familiar grin that I thought I had lost forever.

As I turned away, I smiled to myself. It was good to have John back in some way. Maybe he was more like John than I knew.

I went back to my cabin, but I could not get my mind off of how much he looked like John. He did not look like a pirate or act like one. He was a much more clean-cut, well-educated, straitlaced type of guy. I would have to give him some of John's old clothes.

I dozed off and woke up in my bedroom to the sound of two kids arguing. It was going to be a great day. I could tell already. Miracles do happen.

The kids and I had a great day with no fighting. Occasionally, my mind would escape to the ship, Andre, Christopher, and my promise to John.

That night, the moon was big and bright, and the stars were shining brilliantly. It reminded me of when I was young, and I wished upon a star. I said, "Star light, star bright, please, God, guide me to where I'm supposed to be."

After that, I went to sleep and woke up on the ship. The men were singing in the dining hall when I walked in. They were holding their mugs up and swaying them back and forth while one man played an accordion.

Christopher was wearing an apron in the corner. He must have been told to work in the kitchen.

As I walked to my table, the men greeted me. It was nice to be acknowledged. I sat down in John's old seat.

Christopher came right over with a mug of coffee. He placed the mug on the table and said, "They told me this is what you like to drink."

I looked up at him and felt as though I was looking at John. I asked if he could join me for dinner. He said they had another job for him.

Andre came over and said we were going to sail up the coast of Africa. I had heard rumors the girls might be there. Chills went down my spine at the thought of actually finding John's sisters.

Andre said, "The men like you, Bell. They are glad that you have stayed with us, and they like Christopher too. He reminds them of John."

After dinner, I decided to go to the main deck. I went over to the helm. The crewmen at the wheel let me take over for a few minutes. I started to think about John as I looked out at the water. I asked John if he had left Christopher as a memento for me. I let John know that I would train Christopher as a swordsman. It started to get misty, and I was getting tired. On the way back to my cabin, I saw Christopher.

He said, "I'm glad I met you. Thanks for letting me come along."

In my cabin, everything seemed to remind me of John. I only hoped that I could fulfill the promises I had made to him. I fell asleep and woke up in my bed at home.

I had a lot to do that day, and my kids were going on a family camping excursion with their friends. We had to run around and buy sleeping bags and supplies for the trip. I could not stop thinking about Christopher because he was a reminder of how much I loved John.

My girlfriend called to meet for lunch, and since I was out and about, we met up for a quick lunch. It was nice to catch up with each other. I hadn't seen her since the beginning of my dreams, which seemed like several lifetimes ago. She asked me how everything was. I told her about my dreams. It was hard for me to differentiate between my real life and my dream life. We promised to get together again soon for another lunch date.

I finished my to-do list and went home. That evening, my husband and I had cocktails and talked how the kids were getting older. I thought it was odd when he said that I was changing.

He said, "I don't know if it is good or bad, but I like the changes."

I really did not feel like I was changing. However, I did feel I was becoming my own person. I liked myself more. Maybe since the kids were getting older, I had more time to explore who I was and what I wanted. I knew my dreams helped, but I did not say anything about them to my husband. He wanted to fool around, but I was so exhausted from the day that I just wanted to go right to bed. He understood. I fell asleep quickly because I didn't miss a beat.

I was back on the ship, and it seemed like the middle of the night. I decided to go to the upper deck. I headed toward the bow and saw Christopher reading a book with his feet up.

"Do you always sneak up on people?" he asked.

I said, "No, I did not realize anyone would be up at this hour. I could not sleep. I decided to come up and look around."

He said, "It is a beautiful evening. There are thousands of stars shining bright. It is amazing to see."

We started to talk about John and how different they were.

Christopher said, "John was older by a couple of minutes, but he always treated me as a much younger brother. He always looked out for me when we were growing up. John wanted me to go with him to find our sisters, but I chose to stay with my mother and take care of her. I regret not going with John, and I hope to make up for some of the regret. I hope it's not too late." His eyes filled with tears.

I could tell it was not easy for him to admit, but he was facing it like a man. I was impressed by his courage. I enjoyed his humble honesty. I enjoyed talking to him, just as I enjoyed talking to John.

He said, "You loved my brother."

I said, "Very much." I really did not want to talk about John, and I asked if he had ever been in love.

He said, "Yes, once, but we were very young and afraid, and we never—"

"Oh, so you're a virgin, are you?"

He grinned and said, "Yes, I guess I am."

He was as confident as John, which I found very attractive. After talking to him for a bit longer, I excused myself. He offered to walk me back to my cabin, but I said, "No, finish your book. Good night."

In my cabin, I thought about Christopher and how I enjoyed being with him and talking with him. It felt like I had feelings toward him—similar feelings as I had had for John. I could not understand what I was feeling. *How could I? This is John's brother.* We would find their sisters and everything would change. I just needed to stay focused on my promise to John.

I heard a knock at the door.

Andre brought me coffee and said, "Good morning, Bell. We are headed to the coast of Africa. We have some contacts there. They will be able to help us find the girls ... if they are there. We will be there in just a couple of days. We need to get the men prepared for our mission." He asked how I liked Christopher.

I said I liked him, but he was very different from his brother. John had more confidence and was a leader. Christopher had the potential, but he had a lot to learn.

After Andre left my cabin, I went to the main deck. I went over to the helm and took over the wheel for a little bit. I loved being at the helm. I felt like I was in control, and that felt empowering. I was wearing John's old clothes, but I did not think much about how I looked in the pirate's outfit. The wind was blowing. It was a very beautiful day. I saw dolphins swimming in the water. It was truly amazing to see their beauty. I wondered what would happen once we got to Africa. It was strange. I was not afraid. I knew we could handle whatever came our way. We were strong fighters.

Christopher came up to me with another mug of coffee.

"Thank you," I said.

He sat next to me, propped his feet up, and made himself comfortable. I could tell he wanted to talk. Finally, he said, "Do you think you could ever fall in love again?"

"Why do you ask?"

"I do not know if I ever could fall in love again. It is very scary to have those feelings for someone and for something to destroy it. You are a strong woman. My brother was lucky to have you in his life. I am going to do everything I can to help you keep your promise to my brother."

As usual, I ate dinner in the cabin by myself. I decided to go the main deck after dinner, and I saw Christopher mopping the deck.

"They really have you working, don't they?" I asked. I was looking out at the water. Once again it looked so peaceful.

I felt his hand on my shoulder, and chills went down my spine.

Christopher said, "It won't be long until we get there."

I asked, "Are you feeling sick?"

He said, "No, I'm just getting a little anxious." He looked at the water and then leaned toward me and kissed me.

I got so nervous that I ran back to my cabin. He reminded me of John in so many ways. *What am I doing?* I hugged my pillow. I could not believe the emotions I was feeling. *What is going on with me? This cannot be happening.*

I dozed off and woke up in my bed. A warm breeze blew in through the open window. My husband must have opened it before he left for work that morning. For some reason, I got up with a happy feeling and got the kids up for school. I wondered why my husband had let me sleep late instead of waking me up. I got a lot done that day. It always felt good to get things done and feel productive. I got home from running around all day and started dinner.

When my husband came home, we had cocktails and talked about our day. I asked why he had not woken me up that morning.

He said, "You had a really rough night. I decided to let you sleep a little longer."

We had dinner and got ready for bed. It felt good to get into bed after a long day. The cleaning girl had come that day, and I always slept better with fresh linens on the bed. I was not surprised to find myself back on the ship.

I went up to the main deck. I was standing near the bow when I saw Christopher. I said, "Now who is sneaking up on whom?"

"I didn't hear you, and I have great instincts."

"That will be a tremendous help when you sneak up on your enemies."

It was easy to talk to Christopher. The conversation just seemed to flow. We talked about his and John's childhood. The time had passed so quickly, and I realized it was around noontime. *Where did the morning go?* I said, "We have to teach you how to use a sword."

I asked Andre to help get the men organized and prepare the weapons. Christopher and I went to the stern so I could show him some simple moves. I needed to see what his strong and weak points were and where to begin the lessons.

He held the sword well. I was surprised because he made it seem like he was clueless when it came to sword fighting.

I showed him a couple of fundamental moves that he also picked up very quickly. I was very impressed.

Finally, he confessed that he had been practicing with one of the other crewmen.

When I turned to see who it was, Christopher swatted me on the butt with his sword.

I said, "We will have none of that, Mr. Taylor."

"Okay, then we will practice some more tomorrow."

I could not help but be reminded of John.

"Andre, we have to be prepared if we are going to reach the coast of Africa tomorrow."

Later that evening, I heard a knock on my door. It was Christopher. I invited him into my cabin. A happy feeling came over me. I thought it was a bit strange, but I was happy to feel again. There was a jug of rum on the table, and I offered him a drink.

He said, "Only if you drink with me."

I really did not drink, but I took a sip. I could feel the warmth of the rum going down. It was a soothing feeling. We started talking about our families. I told him all about my father, and he told me all about his.

Before I knew it, I could feel his energy pulling me toward him. I was more than happy to go. We embraced like we were meant to be together, like a force was driving us together. As he kissed my mouth, I could taste how thirsty he was to have me, all of me. I could not hold back my feelings.

I whispered in his ear, "I want you!"

I was caught up in his thirst. On the bed, we held each other. He never stopped looking at me. His eyes had a look of hunger in them, and it wasn't for food; it was for me. I was taken by how beautiful a lover he was. He was incredible. He reminded me of John once more. We made love all night long. We were completely drenched in our sweat, and when I thought he had had enough, he was right back inside of me. He wanted more, and I was more than happy to oblige. We held each other until I woke up.

I immediately heard my kids fighting, and I yelled, "Stop arguing." I could smell the aroma of fresh-brewed coffee in the air. I looked over at my nightstand and saw a cup of coffee. Waking up to a cup of coffee in the morning was one of my favorite things.

I could hear the shower running in the bathroom. *Did I really go through that last night? Christopher was amazing.*

It felt like a new beginning and a renewed sense of love. I could feel that rush you get when you fall in love. I had an exhilarating feeling inside of me, a new touch with love. It was very exciting, but I knew I had to fulfill my promise to John. *Wait a minute. It was a dream! What am I thinking? This is not real.*

I had to get a grip. It was getting out of hand. What was wrong with me? I got the kids off to school and decided to have a day to myself. I had to try to get myself together and maybe make some sense of my dreams.

I ended up at our country club. I sat by the pool and had lunch. The sky was the most gorgeous shade of blue, and there was not a cloud in the sky. Days like that reminded me of when I was young girl and my family would go to the Bahamas in the summertime. It reminded me of Hawaiian Tropic tanning oil, the one with the coconut smell. I loved that smell. It reminded me of the beach, which brought me back to the blue sky. I missed those days of not having a care in the world.

The club was pretty crowded that day. I was not the only one who needed a day to myself. At one point, someone jumped into the pool and splashed me with water. This brought me back to reality. I knew I had been away in my fantasy world because I was thinking about Christopher. I was thinking about how different he was from his brother. John was arrogant and cocky, and Christopher was soft and gentle. I wondered if Christopher was ready for the fight that we were going into. I wondered how long I had been in the fantasy world before I was splashed.

I decided to spend the rest of the day in the sun. I needed to pull myself together. The dreams were taking over my life. I had to figure out what I was doing. *It is not normal. What am I going to do? I suppose this is better than having an actual affair because I am not hurting anyone with my dreams.*

I had to figure out what I needed in my life in order to be happy. I was exhausted from thinking so much and decided to get takeout for dinner.

When my husband got home, he asked what was for dinner. I told him the rotisserie chicken was on the dining room table. He came into the bedroom where I was changing and slapped my butt.

I said, "Hey, the chicken's out there."

He said, "I know. I just had to slap your butt. It looked so cute. What made you get chicken, Rayne?"

I said, "I didn't feel like cleaning up the mess after making dinner."

It was getting close to bedtime, and I could sense that my husband was in the mood to fool around. I went through the motions, but it was not the same as it had been with John or Christopher. It was more of a wifely duty with my husband than the passionate, loving act of two lovers. He asked if I was okay because he sensed the lack of passion too.

I said, "What about your passion?"

We did not speak any further. We never did when it came to issues that might have caused us to open up and be real about what was going on in our lives.

When I woke up, Andre was yelling, "Bell! Bell! We have news of the girl's whereabouts. They have been split up. One of them is going to be sold on the selling block on Saturday morning, and the other was kept for the captain of the slave ship. He has her kept in a cottage about an hour or so outside of town."

Christopher woke up and said, "What's the ruckus all about?"

Andre looked over my shoulder and smiled at me. He asked if I knew what I was doing.

I said, "Yup."

We told Christopher about his sisters. We needed to come up with a plan of attack.

Surprisingly, Christopher came up with a plan. His idea was quite brilliant. The plan was to split into two groups and rescue the girls at the same time. We would go by horseback early Saturday morning and meet back at the ship.

As Andre left to get the plans underway, I heard him mutter, "He is just like his brother."

When we got to the main deck, the men were preparing their weapons and sharpening their swords. The master gunners were cleaning the cannons in case we had some sort of incident on the ship. Everyone was busy. Even Christopher was sharpening his sword. He asked if I would show him some moves with the sword. I quickly pulled out my sword, and he moved back.

I said, "There. I sure got you to move fast."

"Ha Ha," he said. He walked me back to my cabin for some clean clothes. He wanted to stay the night, but I told him we needed our rest for tomorrow. Energy and rest, he understood. I was ready for bed. We had been planning and preparing for the attacks all day. I could not wait to go to sleep.

I woke to my husband getting ready to leave for work. I asked, "You were going to let me sleep?"

"You've been acting strange. I thought you needed to sleep."

"Okay. Thank you. I suppose I have been acting a bit strange," I said.

After he left, I started thinking about my day—paying bills, finding a tutor for the kids, after-school activities, grocery shopping, and doctor's appointments I had to make. The list went on and on. I had to get the kids to school before I could start my day.

I met a friend for lunch between the errands. I love this teahouse we sometimes met at. They have the best soups, finger sandwiches, and scones. I used to bring my daughter there when she was little. She loved to dress up pretending to be a grown up having a special lunch and tea with me. Sipping tea from an antique teacup makes me feel like a lady.

My friend asked about my dreams, but I did not want to talk about them. She would never have believed just how wrapped up I had become in my dreams. It was a little over the top, and I quickly changed the subject to our children.

That night, it was hard to fall asleep. I decided to read for a while

That usually sent me into a deep sleep. The next thing I remembered was being on the ship.

Andre knocked at the door with my morning coffee. *I love this dream!* Andre had sent someone to wake Christopher, but he was already up. Apparently, Christopher had been preparing all night for the rescues. The horses were ready everybodywas ready to go!

Christopher came into my cabin to finalize our plans. We split into groups. We had to have some men stay behind to watch the ship. Andre, and a few others would head toward the selling block. Christopher and I would take a few men and go to the captain's cottage for John and Christopher's other sister. We would ride together until we had to part ways.

I was nervous about riding a horse. I could not remember if I could ride or not. It turned out I could ride horses! *What a surprise! What a great dream.*

Once we parted ways, it took us about an hour of riding to get to the cottage. We were lucky that the weather was nice. We stopped two times for the horses to get water and rest for a minute. Christopher was very serious and focused on our mission. I felt very safe with him. He really stood up and took responsibility, just like his brother would have done. It was clear to me now why I had fallen in love with him.

When we got to the cottage, we watched from a distance to assess the situation. An older man was working in the field. A woman was doing laundry. As we got closer, I could see the tears in Christopher's eyes when he realized it was his sister. We had to hold him back for a minute until we knew it was safe for him to get her.

Once we realized the captain was away from the property, Christopher quietly got Mary's attention. He swept her up on the horse, and we rode away. *That was easy,* I thought.

When we were a few miles away, we stopped so Christopher and Mary could have a few moments together. We all had to find out what she knew about the others.

Christopher had one of the men take Mary back to the ship. She would be safe there while we went to the selling block to help Andre get Sara. I had a feeling it was not going to be quite as easy to get her back. It took us about two hours to get to town.

By the time we arrived in town, it was crowded. I guess it should not have been such a surprise to see a large group of pirates gathered in the town square. Everyone was waiting for the bidding to start. Some of the pirates were drunk and getting impatient. They were yelling all kinds of vulgarities. We spotted Andre. He knew where they were holding the girls. We had to distract the crowd. We would have to create something to draw their attention away from the bidding area.

In the meantime, we told Andre about Mary. We told him she was safely back on our ship. We did not know how much time we had before the captain found out we had taken her from the cottage. We had to work fast to get Sara and anyone else we could rescue. Maybe we could send one of the men back to the ship to get it ready to sail. Andre agreed with that suggestion. We had to get out of there soon with half the men on the ship and the other half in town. We were not prepared to fight the entire town, and we had to move fast. We decided that the horses would be our distraction. I said I would release them into the square. I would just wait for Andre's signal.

I said, "Christopher, you will have to get Sara. The others will follow. Everyone on horseback can carry an extra person. That's the best we can do at this time. I wish we could rescue all the girls, but we do not have enough time."

Andre signaled, and I motioned to Christopher. The horses created so much commotion that no one even noticed Christopher rescuing Sara and the other enslaved girls. I did not expect to see Christopher handle himself in the manner in which he did while rescuing his sister. The other men from our crew followed Christopher's lead by snatching the other girls and putting them on their backs. Everything was happening so fast, but the plan was working. By the time some of the pirates noticed what was happening, we were ready to leave town. Mission accomplished!

From out of nowhere, a pirate stepped in front of Christopher's horse. He raised his sword to slash the horse's throat.

Christopher, without flinching, took the whip he had attached to his hip and swung it so fast that the pirate was on his butt—and off we went! I could not believe how he had handled himself. He was constantly surprising me.

It would take us about an hour to get back to the ship. Hopefully, the crewmen would have everything ready to set sail and pull the anchor.

Andre reassured us that the crew would have everything under control because they were very reliable. We did not realize the captain of the slave ship was coming for Mary. It was midafternoon by the time we arrived back at the ship.

We got the ship moving, and we were off. Behind us, we saw the captain of the slave ship. We readied the weapons, put the girls on the lower deck, and all hell broke loose. The other ship started to fire. They were relentless. They wanted what we took, and they were not leaving until they got it. In the uproar, we did not see the captain board our ship with a couple of other men.

I yelled, "Christopher!"

I had flashbacks of John. *I can't lose Christopher too!*

He said, "Don't worry. I've got this!" He took his whip, lassoed the captain to the ground, and took his knife. Christopher stabbed the captain to death. I think the idea of losing his brother and this man taking his sisters overcame his emotions.

The captain never knew what was coming. When everything was done, the ship sank, but we did not kill the crew. We put them on a rowboat so they would spread the word that Bell of the Sea was here to stay. I would be guarding the seas.

Christopher was with his sisters, and it was wonderful to see them reunited. He introduced them to me, and they were very appreciative of everything we had done for them.

Later on, Christopher and I were talking about our lives and what we wanted. I said, "This is my life now. This was where I belong."

He said, "I belong with you, Bell. There is nowhere else I want to be than with you."

"I want to be with you too, Christopher. I was hoping you would want to stay."

My heart was pounding. I could not believe what I was hearing. I saw his mouth moving, but I could not believe what he was saying.

He said, "We will live this life together."

I think my heart stopped beating as we kissed with such intensity. I knew we would be together forever. That night, we made love. He was good at everything he did, and it was only the beginning. The next thing I knew, I woke up in my bed at home. *Darn!*

CHAPTER 6

All I wanted to do was get back to Christopher and the ship. It was harder and harder to wake up and let go of the dreams. I went through the day and wondered if I would ever see him again. I was in a fog. I could not get myself together. I did not know what I was doing anymore. I did not know what I had gotten myself into with the dreams. I was having affairs with all these men. They were more than affairs though; it felt as though each one had given me something I secretly needed, wanted, and desired in my real life. I could not wait to go to sleep. Maybe I would see Christopher again.

I woke up in a cabin. I knew immediately that I was not on the ship. I was wearing a pair of old jeans and a thin, linen shirt. There were some worn black leather boots near the bed. What am I doing here? I got out of the small bed, walked to the window, and looked out. To the left, I saw swampy water. To the right, I saw a wooded area.

It did not take long to walk through the rest of the cabin because it was rather small. The cabin had one bedroom, a small kitchen, and a living space with a table near the window. It looked like someone had gone to a garage sale and decorated the cabin. It had a wood-burning stove in the kitchen and a pump on the sink for water. In the living area, there was a fireplace. I love a wood-burning fireplace. I had the feeling that maybe there was no electricity because there were lanterns all around the cabin.

I walked outside to get a better feel for where I was. The cabin was at the base of a swampy enclave. There was a river that the enclave branched off of. There was a small dock with a wooden rowboat. Across the river, I could see a huge mansion. It was as pretty as a picture in a magazine for Southern-style living.

In the back, near a wooded area on the property, there was a small stable with a horse, some chickens, a couple of pigs, and a cow. How strange. I knew exactly what to do for these animals. I knew where the feed was, what they needed, and how to take care of them. They had names too! My horse's name was Henry. He had a beautiful shiny chocolate brown coat.

Someone said, "Hello, hello!"

I turned quickly and saw the most gorgeous man on a huge horse. He said, "Finally, I got your attention."

I was a bit dazed. *He thinks he can talk to me like that?*

He said, "Hello, my name is Jarred. I live across the river on the hill."

I said, "I'm Kate."

"Hello, Kate," he said. He was very proper. "Would you like to come over for tea this afternoon?"

Why not? This is a dream. I might as well go.

"I'll show you how to get to my property," he said.

"Okay. Thank you. That sounds lovely."

He told me to go down the road to the bridge and cross over to his property.

"I'll see you in a bit," I said.

"Wonderful," he said.

I went back to my cabin, washed up, and went to see Jarred.

When I arrived at the bridge, I could not believe how magnificent his mansion was. It reminded me of a plantation. *Maybe it is a plantation.* His home was a majestic, two-story white mansion with huge pillars. A middle-aged, thin, properly dressed black man greeted me.

He said, "Miss Kate, I'm Cartwright. Mr. Townsend is expecting you in the parlor."

Cartwright took me to the parlor, which was very large with a beautiful fireplace as the focal point of the room. The fireplace was huge large enough to walk inside! It was only about a minute or two before Jarred came into the room. I was taken aback by how beautiful he was. He had stunning blue eyes and dark wavy hair. He was a sight to behold. I was taking it all in without hesitation. He looked at me and said, "Do you always wear riding clothes?"

I answered curtly, "It was short notice."

We stayed in the parlor, and a woman brought us tea and pastries.

He asked how long I had lived in Louisiana.

I said, "A couple of years."

He said, "I have seen you, but I never could get your attention."

"What about you? How long have you lived here?" I asked.

"I was born and raised here in the bayou."

"Have you always lived in this home?"

"Yes. I grew up on this plantation. I breed and raise horses and dabble in banking. Next week, I'm having a party. Would you like to come?"

I said, "I would love to."

He said, "It's going to be formal … so don't wear riding clothes. You might feel a little out of place."

I smiled and replied, "What's wrong with riding clothes?"

In my mind, I heard him speak, but all I could think about was his muscular body and his gorgeous smile. I suddenly realized it was getting dark. Funny, it seemed like I had just gotten there, but we had been talking for hours.

I said, "Oh my, I have to go. Jasper is delivering my mail and some supplies, and I don't want to miss him. He comes once a week by boat." As I rushed out, I said, "I'll see you next week at the party."

As I approached my cabin, I could hear Jasper's dinghy coming down the waterway.

He yelled, "Kate!"

I ran down to the dock to see what the urgency was.

He said, "Kate, I have news. Some men escaped from the prison last night … about five of them. Keep your gun loaded and watch out for yourself. I'll stay with you if you would like."

"No," I said. "I'll be fine. Thanks, Jasper."

Jasper had lived in Louisiana for his entire life. He had never wanted much, and he would give you the shirt off his back. He looked much older than his years due to being in the sun his whole life. Life in the bayou was rough if you did not have money, but it was perfect in many ways for me because I was by myself. I realized why I lived by myself in the cabin. A few years earlier, I had been heartbroken and left to be alone. I had been living there ever since. I must have been getting over the heartbreak because Jarred took my breath away.

I sat in a rocking chair on the porch. While looking at the mail, I thought about the party and what I was going to wear. I did not think I had anything that would be appropriate. I would have to check my closet. I saw a few pair of jeans and some shirts. There was one dress hidden in the back of the closet. The white dress was beautiful but a bit matronly. I could make some changes to the neckline so it would be more flattering.

I thought about the inmates and loaded my rifle. I went out to the rocking chair on the porch, propped my legs up onto the wood railing, and thought about Jarred. *Why isn't he married? Why did I choose this area to live by myself?*

All of these thoughts were running through my head, and I must have fallen asleep because I woke up in my bed. My two kids were yelling at each other. I was back.

I got up quickly, threw my robe on, and went to the kitchen. I yelled, "That's enough. I'll get breakfast ready while you guys get ready for school."

It occurred to me while I was making breakfast that my husband had not woken me up that morning. *What is up with that?*

I dropped the kids at school just before the bell rang. I hoped they would make it to their homerooms in time. I think they had reached their limit on being tardy. The high school was very strict. They did not put up with any bull. They kept the kids in line, which I liked. They needed restrictions at that age.

I started thinking about my husband again. *Why didn't he wake me?* I went home and started doing laundry. I made a list of everything I wanted to get done. The pool area was at the top of my list, and I started out there first. I immediately went for the bleach. When I spray bleach around, it makes the patio smell fresh. It took most of the day to clean the outside. I was wiped out.

I was happy that the kids got a ride home from school. It made it much easier for me to continue what I was doing instead of stopping to pick them up from school. *When I stop what I'm doing, I lose enthusiasm for the job.*

The sun was starting to set. I had to sit and relax for a few minutes. My mind immediately went to the Louisiana bayou.

How did I end up there? It was very strange. I started thinking about Jarred. I could not wait to see what would happen with this dream. *Why am I having so many dreams about romance? It is very exciting.* I started thinking about the inmates, and chills went down my spine.

The phone rang. It was my husband.

I asked him why he didn't wake me that morning.

He said, "I know you had a lot to do today since we are having my business partners over for dinner tonight. I don't know if you are aware of it, but you toss and turn in your sleep a lot lately. You're so restless. I thought I'd do you a favor and let you sleep."

I had completely forgotten about the business dinner, but the house was clean, especially the pool area. "Let's cook out tonight. We can have steaks on the grill."

He agreed with my suggestion because his partners love steak.

"Great. I'll run to the store and get the steaks. I'll get something for the kids to eat separately so we can have an adult dinner."

He said, "I'll get flowers."

I love fresh flowers. I was so caught up with my dreams that I forgot what was happening in my real life. *This is ridiculous. I really have to get myself together.*

I went to the grocery store and rushed to get everything I needed. I picked up fried chicken for the kids. *They will be happy since it is not Mom's cooking!*

While checking out, I saw my girlfriend. She said, "I have to tell you about this great dream I had last night."

I said, "I have to tell you about mine, but I have to run right now. We are having company, and I'm running late. I'll call you tomorrow. I want to hear all about it."

I arrived home and quickly prepared everything. I had about forty minutes before our guests arrived.

My husband put his special grilling apron on, and I placed the flowers in the center of the table. They looked beautiful. I placed candles all around. *I love the soft glow of candlelight. It is very relaxing—and romantic. Everything looks great.*

I watched my husband prepare the steaks for the grill. *He is a beautiful man. What is wrong with us? Why don't I get excited about our relationship anymore? There was a time when there was no other place I would rather be than by his side. He was all I needed. Our relationship was all I ever needed.*

Have we grown so far apart that we can't go back to that feeling again? Did time steal our love? What about raising a family? Did those years of all work and not enough play finally catch up to us? I feel so lost and afraid. I don't know where we are headed.

The doorbell rang, and I went to get the door. They all arrived together. It was nice to see everyone. It had been months since we all had gotten together. They loved the idea of a cookout.

George and Mae were our age, and Henry and Grace were about fifteen years older. Henry and Grace both looked very youthful.

While I was talking to Mae, I noticed a gleam in her eye as she looked at my husband.

When she realized that I saw what was going on, she quickly looked away.

I could feel my blood pressure rise. I felt very jealous.

After our company left, I took a quick shower.

When I got out, my husband pulled me close. He said, "We need to get closer. Something is missing."

I said, "I feel the same way."

He was too tired to make love. That was fine with me because I wanted to get back to my dream. *It's so hard to live two lives,* I thought.

I fell asleep pretty fast and woke up in the rocking chair on my porch in the bayou. I must have fallen asleep in the rocking chair without realizing. I could hear the birds chirping as I woke up. Sounds in the morning are much more amplified than they are later in the day. I saw squirrels playing around the big oak tree. I saw Henry in the field outside the barn. He must have let himself out of the gate again. He knows how to unlatch the gate with his nose. He is so smart.

After I washed my face and brushed my teeth, I got dressed and started my chores. I fed the animals and got everything done by midmorning.

Jarred's housekeeper walked by the pasture.

"Sara, hello," I said.

"Hello, Miss Kate. It's nice to see you again. I was hoping I would see you. I wanted to tell you that you put a spark in Master Jarred's eye."

I said, "Oh." I got shivers all over my body. I told her to watch out for the inmates. I let her know they were in this area.

She said, "My friend has a rifle, and she's used it a time or two."

I have a rifle too, and I'm not afraid either. I'll be all right. I cannot believe she said I put a spark in Jarred's eye. He definitely put a spark inside of me, which was something I thought I could never feel again. It was good to know I could feel something for someone again. When you have been hurt, it is difficult to open yourself up and trust your heart again. I am going fishing tomorrow. Maybe I will bring Jarred some fish. I started thinking about that dress and what I should do to make it more flattering. When I am finished with my chores, I will see what I can do to spruce it up.

That evening, I listened to the sounds of wildlife outside. It was very peaceful. I had my loaded shotgun next to my bed. I also kept a lantern burning in the window. I don't know if that was for my comfort or to keep the inmates away. *A lantern won't stop them if they want to come into my cabin.*

I must have fallen asleep. I woke up to my daughter screaming that my son took her cell phone and was reading her text messages. Here we go again.

"It's going to be sunny and warm with a chance of rain," the weatherman on the television said.

Amazingly, I got the kids to school on time! I called my friend, and we decided to meet for lunch. I relaxed and took my time getting ready. I am always rushing. I just wanted to take my time and feel good. I took a bubble bath, fixed my hair, and wore makeup. When I was done putting myself together, I looked in the mirror and thought, *I am beautiful. I am desirable. Why doesn't my husband find me desirable anymore?*

My friend and I met at a popular restaurant near the water. She told me about her dreams, and I told her about mine. I did not get into specific details about the dreams. I just shared that they were about romance and excitement.

She told me about her dream. She had gotten married, and her husband was very poor.

We both chuckled because we knew how important money was to her. She always said how she wanted to marry someone with a lot of money. She said, "Maybe my dream is trying to teach me a lesson: that money isn't everything."

I told her about my dreams. I told her about all the romance, the love, and the passion.

She liked my dreams. She said, "I want to dream like that."

After lunch, I went home, got some laundry done, and started to prepare dinner.

When my husband got home, he said, "We are taking a trip north."

I said, "What?"

He said, "You heard me. We are getting away."

I said, "I don't have the proper clothes to just get away. The kids need stuff too."

He handed me a check for two thousand dollars and said, "Go buy what you need."

I could not believe what was happening. It had been so long since we had gotten away. It was exciting to have something to look forward to apart from my dreams.

That night, as I was reading in bed, I thought about my marriage. *I hope I can find out what is missing in our relationship.*

He came into our bedroom and said, "Let's get romantic."

Romantic? Honey, you don't know how to be romantic!

I must have fallen asleep because I woke up in the bayou. The sun was coming up, and it was so beautiful to see the sun rise through the trees. I wanted to get an early start and go fishing. I was able to get my chores done quickly, and I was off. *I sure hope I catch enough catfish to take to Jarred.*

It was a great day for fishing. I caught about a dozen fish. It was perfect I had enough to keep some for myself and plenty to take to Jarred. I cleaned and filleted the fish that I was keeping for myself. Someone must have been cooking possum stew. I could smell the aroma as I was cleaning the fish. When I was finished filleting the fish, I freshened myself up, got Henry ready, and trotted over to Jarred's house. It seemed odd to call it a house when it was clearly a mansion.

On my way over the bridge, I spotted Jarred riding on his property. He came right over to me with a big grin and a puzzled look. I told him I had gone fishing and was bringing him some catfish.

His smile got even bigger, and he said, "Splendid. Let's go up to the house and get them cleaned up. I'm so glad you came over. I did not expect to see you until the party. This is a very pleasant surprise!"

Cartwright brought us some tea and cake while we chatted in the parlor.

Jarred told Cartwright he could have some fish for himself. I could tell by his smile that he appreciated that.

Once again, I felt shivers going through my body as I sat with Jarred. I really enjoyed being around him. He made me feel something I had not felt in a long time.

When we were through with our cake and tea, he showed me around his house. It was quite beautiful and full of the history of his family. The last room he showed me was his bedroom. His mahogany four-poster bed was draped in red velvet. It was fit for a king. *King Jarred,* I thought.

He sat down on his bed and waved for me to sit by his side. In real life, I would have resisted, but since it was a dream, I went right over and sat beside him. My heart started pumping. I tried to act normal, but it was not working. I think he could sense how nervous I was because he grabbed my hand and caressed my face just before he leaned over and kissed me. I started to feel a bit more relaxed.

I could not have imagined how good a kisser he was until he kissed me with his warm, wet, soft lips. His lips were gliding all over my lips, face, neck, and shoulders. *Oh my God. Is this really happening?* He kissed me and undressed me, and before I knew it, we were making love in his bed. I felt like I was on a cloud. It was unbelievable how our bodies molded together and became one. It was like a dance—slow and easy—and he definitely was the leader. It was the most beautiful experience I had ever had. We repeated the dance all night long until we both were so physically exhausted that we could not dance any longer. We held each other, stared into each other's eyes, and fell asleep. *He has the most beautiful blue eyes. I can see forever in them, and I love that look.*

I smelled fresh-brewed coffee, and I opened my eyes. My husband was standing there with a cup of coffee and a huge grin.

I immediately sat up, took the coffee, and asked him why he was smiling.

He said, "You don't know?"

I said, "No."

"Last night ring a bell?"

"Last night? What are you talking about?"

He said, "It was the best lovemaking we have ever had. It was awesome. You turned to me in the middle of the night—and that is when it all began." He seemed so happy as he kissed me good-bye and went off to work.

I yelled, "Have a great day!" *I was with Jarred last night, and it was fantastic. What is going on?* I decided to stay home and do nothing. I needed some time to relax and get my head on straight. I stayed in bed and thought about the previous night. All I could think about was being with Jarred. *How was I with my husband? I have got to get myself together. This is getting crazy. My life is getting more and more confusing. I need to do something with my life. I have to figure out what I need.*

My mind drifted to my dreams, and I wondered where I would wake up that night. Reality hit me, and I started thinking about my kids. I got out of bed and drove them to school.

When I returned home, I had a lot of laundry and cleaning up to do. There was no time to relax with piles of laundry and dishes in the sink, but that didn't stop my mind from drifting to my dreams.

The doorbell rang, but I hadn't been expecting anyone. When I opened the door and saw a beautiful bouquet of flowers, I was quite surprised. The card read, "Enjoyed last night. Love, Michael."

When Michael got home, we had a wonderful dinner as a family. It was rare because everyone seemed to be doing his or her own thing lately. Life can be a bit crazy with everyone having different schedules. Michael works late, and the kids have their activities. I had planned dinner every night, but that didn't mean we ate together.

It was getting time for bed, and I decided to open the window. A warm breeze relaxed me as I fell asleep. I woke up in the morning, and I could hear noises. I wasn't sure where I was. *Are the kids fighting? What is going on?*

As my thoughts and vision got clearer, I realized I was alone in Jarred's bed. I was naked, but I grabbed one of his robes. As I went to look for him, I heard men asking who else was in the house.

Jarred said, "There is no one else in the house. I live here alone." I tiptoed back into Jarred's room. *What should I do?* I quickly got dressed and saw a shotgun above the mantel. Luckily, it was loaded. I was trying to figure out how to get downstairs without being seen or heard. There was a patio outside of Jarred's room which had stairs to the ground level. I quickly got myself together and went to the first floor. I could hear the men. They meant business.

I had never heard such vulgar language. I was trying to peek through the window to see what was happening. They had tied up Cartwright, and they were talking to Jarred and one of his servants. They were in the parlor and demanding whiskey.

Jarred told Sara to get the whiskey glasses. The convicts were restless, but I figured maybe they would relax. After a few drinks, they started to get drunk. They wanted something to eat, and they told Sara to bring them some food.

This is my only chance to help. I got Sara's attention, and she hid me in the pantry. It was clear that she was very upset. I motioned for her to calm down.

One of the men came into the kitchen and grabbed Sara. "I'm gonna have a piece of this."

She pleaded with him not to hurt her.

He said, "You're gonna like what I'm gonna give to you, lady." He dragged her into the back room. She pleaded with him not to hurt her.

I tiptoed out of the pantry and was able to go behind them.

He was on top of her and too busy to notice me.

I didn't want to shoot the gun and bring attention to this area of the house. I turned the gun upside down and hit him as hard as I could with the handle.

He passed out on top of Sara. I dragged him to the pantry, tied him up, and told Sara to bring out the food and act like nothing had happened.

She got herself together and did what I'd said.

One of the men wanted more whiskey, and Jarred told Sara to get another bottle.

I was trying to get a view of the room and the men who were with Jarred and Cartwright. Only four men were left. Two of the men were looking out the window, one had a gun pointed at

Jarred, and the other was doing all the talking. He asked Jarred where he kept his money and his gold. They had heard he was a banker who kept a lot of cash and valuables in the house.

The whiskey was going down fast, and I could see a window of opportunity before they started to get rowdy.

One of the men asked about the guy who I had tied up. Sara said he needed to use the bathroom. The guy chuckled, and his face turned red. It was a bit strange that it would embarrass him.

The guy asking the questions became annoyed with Jarred. He started pushing Jarred around and knocked him to the ground. It seemed odd that Jarred would let the men push him around. It's not like he was a total wimp. He was very strong and capable of defending himself. There had to be some reason why he was not fighting back.

I caught his eye, and he saw my gun. He glanced over at a picture over the mantel. He started to walk toward the mantel when some guy pushed him to the ground.

What are you doing? I'm going to get that guy. I can't believe how mean he is.

Jarred said, "I'm trying to get to my vault. It's over the mantel."

The guy rushed over to see if Jarred was telling the truth. He checked the mantel. No safe. He started to get angry and pushed Jarred around some more.

Jarred said, "The safe is behind the picture. He pushed the picture away and exposed a large safe that was set into the stonewall.

The man said, "Open it."

Jarred looked at me and grinned as he started to open the safe.

What does he have planned?

Jarred opened the safe, pulled out a gun, and started shooting. He took the two guys who were near him, and I took the two lookouts.

Sara ran over to Cartwright and untied him. It all happened so fast. I could not believe it was over.

Jarred came over and held me. He said, "I can't believe we pulled this off. You read my mind from the very beginning. I was hoping that you would get the shotgun from my bedroom. You read my mind. Everything was perfect ... just like you."

By the time the sheriff's arrived, it was nighttime. The officers took the convicts away. He could not believe we had survived. He said, "These men are rapists and murderers with lifetime prison sentences." He thanked us for our courage and for making the bayou safe again.

Jarred said, "It was Kate. She had all the courage for everyone." He winked at me and smiled.

After the sheriff's left, I told Jarred I needed to go home.

He said, "Are you sure you don't want to stay?"

I said, "I really need to get home."

He said, "Okay, but I'm going to take you."

We got to the cabin, and he checked to make sure everything was safe. He kissed me and said, "Are you sure you don't want me to stay?"

I said, "I'm sure."

He kissed me again and said, "I'll see you tomorrow night at the party. I can't wait to show you off to everyone and tell them how you saved my life."

Once he left, I felt like I was in a daze. *Did this day really happen?* The cabin seemed so small after being in Jarred's home, but I was comfortable. It was my cabin, my taste, and my things. It was good to be home. I got in bed, stared at the ceiling, and recollected the day. I could not believe what had happened. It felt like a dream within a dream.

I woke up to commotion. I said, "What is going on?"

My husband said, "We are going camping. Come on. It will be fun. We haven't done anything spontaneous in so long. It is just for the weekend."

We had everything we needed in the garage, including pop-up tents and sleeping bags. All we had to do was go to the grocery store for food and supplies. *I do not know what is going on with my husband. He planned a trip north. He planned this camping trip this weekend. Maybe he realizes that time has passed us by—and he is trying to make up for lost time.*

Before I knew what was going on, we had arrived at our camping destination. We set up camp and started a fire. It was wonderful to realize that our family was really enjoying each other's company!

We set up camp near the lake so the kids could fish. *Maybe we will catch some fish for dinner.*

My son yelled that they had caught a fish. *Guess who gutted and cleaned the fish?*

My husband was impressed with my ability to clean and fillet the fish. He asked where I learned to do it.

I said, "In a dream."

He just smiled and gave me a strange look.

I have adored the smell of a campfire since I was a young child. It brings back wonderful memories from when I spent time with my family as a young girl. I miss those days so much. I wish I could go back there just for a day. I hope my kids have fond memories of their childhood too.

After a long day, I went to my tent to go to sleep.

My husband said, "I'm going to stay out here and look at the stars for a bit."

From the tent, I could hear the crackling of the fire. *I love being here. The air is fresh and clean, and the fish was delicious. Everything is so perfect.*

The next thing I knew, I heard birds chirping and a horse neighing. *What is a horse doing in our campground?*

I realized I was no longer in a tent. I was in my cabin in the bayou. I was surprised to be back. I thought that dream was over. *Did all that really happen with the convicts?* I chuckled to myself and made coffee.

The sun was shining so brightly through the window. I decided to sit on the porch and enjoy the morning sunshine. It was a beautiful morning. The bluebirds were singing, the squirrels were playing, and my coffee was perfect. The air was fresh, and the sky was blue. It was good to be back. *I love the way I feel here in the bayou. I love the simplicity.*

The cypress trees were hauntingly beautiful. Some looked like driftwood sticking out of the water, and some were full of foliage and covered with moss. It is amazing to watch the sun rise and set through the trees. They had a glow to them, almost like an aura around them.

While I was sipping my coffee on the porch, Sara walked up and said, "Kate! I just wanted to bring you some of my famous pecan pie. My friend brought pecans back from Baton Rouge. I picked them up the other day when I went to visit her, and I baked this pie especially for you—to thank you for rescuing me from that horrible man."

"Sara, I'm glad I could help." I invited her in for some fresh-brewed coffee and we had some of her famous pecan pie. It was perfect. I said, "Now I see why your pie is famous. It is delicious. You are going to have to give me the recipe."

She said, "I just have to tell you that Mr. Jarred is walking on cloud nine. He is so excited. He doesn't know what to do with himself."

I responded, "About what?"

"He is excited about you, silly! He is just head over heels for you."

My heart started beating really fast. *I feel the same for him, but I cannot share this with Sara.* I said, "Oh, Sara, while you're here, can you take a look at my dress and tell me what you think?"

She said, "I'd love to."

I went to my closet and pulled it out.

She said, "It looks nice, but let me see it on you."

I put the dress on and walked out to where she was.

She turned to me and said, "Darlin', you are gonna be the belle of the ball in that dress. I'm gonna have to scrape Mr. Jarred off the floor tonight."

Sara was a very petite and very beautiful black girl. I thought Cartwright was her father, but I was not sure since it was a dream.

"Miss Kate, I shouldn't tell, but I know Mr. Jarred has something special planned for you this evening. He has a surprise for you. I have got to go now before I say another word."

Surprise? What in the world could she be talking about? I'll just have to wait until tonight to find out.

It was still early. I had the whole day before the party. I decided to go swimming in the river. I knew a safe spot where I wouldn't have to worry about any unwelcome reptiles.

The water was refreshingly cold. It was so invigorating, and it always made my skin look refreshed. I saw Jasper cruising by. I waved, but I don't think he saw me.

I went back to the house and relaxed. I fed the animals and checked on Henry. He must have let himself out again because he wasn't in his stall. I tried to figure out how I was going to ride Henry over to Jarred's in my dress. It wouldn't be easy. *Oh well. I guess I'll worry about that later.*

As I was getting ready, I started thinking about Jarred and how much I enjoyed being with him. *He makes me feel very comfortable; it is as if we have known each other our whole lives. That is one reason why I love him so much. Did I just say love? Yes, I did. I guess I do love him. I just never thought I could love anyone again. I love Jarred. That sounds so weird to me. Okay, then. It might sound weird, but it feels right.*

I finished getting ready, and I was quite surprised at how beautiful I looked. It had been a long time since I had dressed up. I forgot how nice it felt to look at myself and feel good.

I could not believe it when I went to get Henry. Cartwright was sitting outside with a horse and buggy. *This must be my surprise. How nice. I feel like a princess going to a ball.*

He looked at me and said, "Your carriage, miss."

I looked at him and smiled. "Why, thank you, sir."

We both giggled.

When we pulled up to the house, it was all lit up like a Christmas tree.

I said, "Cartwright, I have never seen anything like this in my life. It's beautiful."

He said, "Well, when Mr. Jarred has a party, he goes all out."

I was so glad I had the dress because everyone was dressed like they were going to a ball. The women were dressed so elegantly, and the men were dashing.

When I walked into the party, everyone was in the parlor. They must have removed the furniture because it was standing room only. The home had been transformed into a huge ballroom. Servants were serving drinks and appetizers, and music was playing in the other room.

When I saw Jarred looking at me, my heart started to pound in my chest. *Calm down. Relax.* Everyone was looking at me. *Oh my. Is something wrong with me?*

Jarred came right over to me and reassured me that I was okay. "You look like heaven. You are so beautiful." My nerves relaxed as he took my hand and helped me down the steps into the ballroom. He looked incredible, but more importantly, he was always the perfect gentlemen. He introduced me to everyone at the party and never left my side. He seemed proud to be with me. He was telling everyone how I saved his life.

He asked if I would like to dance, and I didn't have to say a word. He knew my answer by the look in my eyes, and he led me to the other room.

We were dancing to a romantic waltz. All the doors were open in the candlelit room. It was like a scene out of a movie. He was charming and attentive, and I was in complete submission to anything he wanted.

He whispered in my ear, "Can I keep you?"

I said, "What?"

He said, "How would you like to spend the rest of your life with me?"

I looked at him with tears in my eyes. I could not believe what he was saying. I looked into his soft, clear, blue eyes, and I knew there was no place I'd rather be than by his side. I said, "Yes. Yes with all my heart. Yes."

He kissed me with the most adoring kiss. His smile said everything. His beautiful blue eyes said everything.

A strangely familiar feeling came over me. *I am home. Jarred is my home. Jarred is my true love, the one I dreamed of as a young girl, the one I waited for my whole life.* I stood there with tears in my eyes as my childhood memories flooded my mind. I could not believe what was happening. Everything I buried long ago was being dug up all over again.

Jarred got everyone's attention and said, "I just asked Kate to marry me, and she said yes!"

Everyone started clapping and congratulating us.

This is so wonderful. What a beautiful surprise. I can't imagine anything better. I knew my true love would come for me.

Jarred turned to kiss me, and I woke up just like that.

CHAPTER 7

ૐ

It startled me when I woke up in the tent. I was so caught up with Jarred and that feeling of finally being home that I almost thought the dream was real. I wished the dream was real, but the familiar smell of fresh-brewed coffee brought me right back to the family camping trip.

This must be the end of my dreams. I finally found my Mr. Right.

I could smell bacon and hear the kids yelling, "We want to go fishing!"

My husband yelled, "I'm cooking breakfast. After breakfast, we will go fishing."

When I came out of the tent, my husband handed me a cup of coffee. It made me happy to see us acting like a family. It had been so long since we had been together, enjoying each other's company.

He asked if I wanted to go fishing with them after breakfast. They were going to go near a waterfall.

I said, "Would you mind if I just stay in the sun by the lake?"

He seemed a little disappointed, but he understood. He did not say anything. I think he just wanted to enjoy himself and relax too.

He said, "All right, but you have to cook and clean the fish when we get back."

I said, "Okay. That sounds fair."

I did not realize how tired I was. I fell asleep on the lounge chair and woke to my husband and the kids laughing and joking about who caught the most trout.

Yeah! Trout is my favorite! I said, "I'll clean the fish. Honey, you can cook them since you are the better outdoor cook."

He said, "No, no. You said you would clean them and cook them. It's only fair that you do what you said you would."

I said, "I don't mind cleaning, but you are the better outdoor cook. I think it's only right that you cook the fish."

He said, "I'm only teasing. The kids are going to clean them, and I'll cook them."

I said, "What can I do?"

He said, "You can make the salad. There are tomatoes and lettuce in the cooler."

I said, "Great. If you would like, I will rinse and scale the fish while you guys get cleaned up."

I could feel a chill come over me while I was rinsing the fish. I must have gotten sunburned. *I love being here. It is so peaceful and relaxing. The weather is perfect, and the scenery is magnificent. It feels like I am in one of my dreams on this trip. It makes me sad to think that we have to leave tomorrow. I would like time to stop so we could live in this moment forever, but time doesn't stop. These moments are so precious, and they slip through our fingers like sand. Life truly is bittersweet. I am grateful for this wonderful life that we have together—no matter what the outcome is.*

We ate dinner at five o'clock, which gave us the rest of the evening to relax with a glass of wine and watch the sunset. Watching all the colors in the sky change was romantic and beautiful. We complimented each other on the delicious dinner. The fish was cooked perfectly, and the salad was crisp and fresh. Everything was perfect.

My husband said, "It's too bad we don't have any privacy. It would be wonderful to make love on a night like this."

I've had enough love lately. I could use the break, but now that I think of it, it would be nice. From the tent, I could hear crickets as I fell asleep.

Much to my surprise, I woke up in an office. I looked at myself. I was wearing a beige outfit and a straw hat with a drawstring. I could not figure out what I was doing, but I was hoping it would come to me.

I was not alone. There were several men in the office, too.

One of them said, "Are you ready, Beth?"

I said, "Yes, Jake." *Oh my. I know his name? That is odd.* I quickly looked on top of the desk to see if it would give me a clue about what I was doing there. A laptop was open to a picture of me with some guys on a volcano. *I think it is the guys in this room. We are all dressed in beige outfits and straw hats. It looks like we are explorers of some sort.* On the walls, there were pictures of artifacts we had found. We were carrying shovels and looking at maps. By the looks of things, we were archeologists.

The newspaper clippings on the walls said my name was Elizabeth McClure. *I must be called Beth. I prefer the name Elizabeth.*

They were loading up a van with all the tools we needed for the expedition. I could see them through the window.

Someone said, "We're ready to go."

This is really happening. We really must be explorers because there is nobody here I am interested in. I hope I'm not the project planner on this expedition because I don't have a clue about where we are going or what we are doing. I'll lay low. I hope that it's all going to come to me.

As we were driving, the guys started joking about how I almost fell into the volcano. They were laughing about how they had to save me from falling into it.

"Hey, Beth," one of the men said. "We hope you don't fall off the mountain on this expedition!"

What am I doing here?

We pulled into a small airport. A private jet was waiting to take us to our destination. While we were waiting for the pilot to arrive, a man walked up to us.

I dropped my bag, which had my camera, a notepad, and a few other essentials. I said, "Oops. Can you pick that up for me?"

He snapped at me and said, "I'm not your servant."

I looked up and saw the most beautiful blue eyes staring at me. I said, "Who are you?"

He said, "The pilot."

"Oh, hello. I'm Elizabeth McClure."

"It's nice to meet you," he said. "I know who you are."

"Well, do you have a name—or should I refer to you as the pilot?"

"It's a pleasure to meet you, Elizabeth. I'm Chase Anderson. Are you and your crew ready to take off?"

I felt a spark of electricity go through my body as he said his name. *Here we go,* I thought. *I found my true love already. Who is this? I guess we will have to see what's in store for Beth, huh?*

We loaded up the plane and took off.

I was relieved that it was a sunny day. I hated to fly in bad weather. I hated to fly at all.

Someone had brought me a drink and a sandwich, which was very thoughtful.

I don't care how gorgeous that man is. He is rude. What is up with him? Does he know who I am? What am I saying? I don't even know who I am. I dozed off and thought about where the dream was going to take me. *What else is there to dream about? I've found my true love. What else can there be for me? Will there be something more than finding my true love?*

When I woke up, my husband was looking at me with a cup of coffee in his hand. Everything was ready to go except the tent. We were packed up and on the road in no time.

My husband put his hand on my lap and said, "It is wonderful to be together. It has been a long time since we had quality time together."

We got home at about noon, which was perfect. We must have been having a heat wave or something. It was absolutely scorching outside. Even with air-conditioning blasting at sixty degrees, the heat in the car was unbearable! *I can't imagine what the house is going to feel like because we turned the air conditioner off before we left for the weekend.*

My husband said, "Stay in the car and relax. I'll go put the air on in the house and get it cooled off for you."

That is so sweet. How considerate of him!

When I got into the house, I plopped down on the lounge sofa in the den. It felt wonderful after a weekend of roughing it.

My husband said, "Did the weekend wear you out? I hope not. Let me get you some lunch. Stay right there. Keep your feet up." He got right on the telephone and ordered lunch. *He is my kind of man.*

It was nice to get home and not have to worry about anything. My husband unpacked the car and took care of everything. *What has gotten into him? He is being so sweet.*

The rest of the day went by very smoothly. When it was time for bed, my husband wanted to stay up to finish watching a football game. I kissed him good night and went to bed.

I woke up on the plane. I put my glasses on and read my notes. I was hoping to get some ideas about what we were doing and where we were going.

Some sort of solid gold snake statue and other primitive relics, which are very sacred to the natives of the island, are in a cave beside a mountain. I have arranged to meet with a native guide who will bring us to our destination. I found newspaper clippings about our other expeditions. I am a famous archeologist, and my men and I only do high-profile sites. *That explains the private jet.*

All of a sudden, the pilot came out of the cockpit.

I looked at him and gasped. "What are you doing out here? Who is flying the plane?"

He said, "I have it on autopilot. I just wanted to get a cup of coffee."

He acts as if I think I'm better than him or something. I can tell by the way he talks to me with that sarcastic tone. I have never in my life … who does he think he is? I'm nice. I haven't been rude, have I?

Chase went back to the cockpit, and a few minutes later, he informed us that we would be descending in just a few minutes. "Prepare for landing … and put on your seat belts, please."

It is not my imagination. I know sarcasm when I hear it.

I looked out of the window toward the mountain. *This is not going to be an easy hike to the cave. The jungle surrounding the mountain looks very dense. I hope we packed machetes. We will need them.*

It was a bumpy landing, but we landed, which made me happy. *I don't like to fly. Why did I choose this career?*

Chase exited the plane and helped everyone off. When it was my turn, he looked at me, bowed, stuck out his hand, and lowered his head like I was royalty.

We looked at each other and smiled.

I felt my knees go weak. *Even though he is sarcastic and rude, he is a good-looking man.*

He asked if he could come along on the expedition.

I said, "If you can handle it, you can come."

He said, "All right. I think I can hold my own."

Sarcasm, I thought.

The next thing I knew, Chase was carrying a big gun.

I said, "What do you need that for?"

He said, "I like to be prepared."

I looked at him like he was crazy—but okay.

Our guide was tall, dark, and had a very serious look on his face. He wore jeans, a T-shirt, and sneakers. He said, "Elizabeth McClure, it's so good to meet you. I am Nigel Tomo. We have a couple of miles of hiking ahead of us. I want to get everybody to the cave before dark."

Once we started our journey into the jungle, everybody else pulled out machetes. *Looks like I didn't get the memo. I like this dream. I don't have any idea where it's going, but I like it.*

The jungle was hot, but oddly there was no humidity. Being from Florida, I knew all about humidity. This is a dream!

Nigel led the way. Chase stayed by my side, and the others surrounded me. I felt like royalty again.

After about a mile and a half, Nigel turned to me and said, "Let's rest for a few minutes. We don't have much farther to go."

Chase suggested setting up camp outside the cave, and everyone agreed that would be best. That way, we would not have to journey back and forth through the jungle.

When we finally reached the open area, stones outlined the perimeter. It looked as though people had ceremonious gatherings there. A huge snake was carved into the mountain just outside the cave. *I did not expect this. I do not know what I had in my head, but it was not this.* I looked at Nigel and said, "Do you want to tell me something?"

He looked at me and said, "Okay. I didn't tell you everything about the statue."

I said, "Really? Would you like to share with me now?"

"The statue is worshiped among my people, and a huge python protects the statue and the people of this island. It is an old superstition, but we believe it. We do not question it. Every year, as an act of faith, we sacrifice a child of one the families. This year, it is my family's turn. My daughter is the sacrifice. Whoever is sent into the cave and comes out alive after a week will be protected by the Gods. Nobody has ever survived. But if she dies, then she was meant to die. The sacrifices will continue.

"I brought you here to kill the snake and save my daughter. I thought of you because I know you will bring no harm to our island. You have an impeccable reputation in your studies of primitive treasures. If I told you the truth, you would not have come. I had to do this for my family. I figured everyone could win here."

Chase said, "I heard about this ritual, but I never imagined it was real."

Nigel said, "It is very real, and my people are very serious about this act of sacrifice. They will not welcome you here. That is why we must hurry. They are preparing my daughter for the sacrifice on the other side of the island. It takes a few days to get here from the other side. This is the last stop of the ceremony. As a sign of devotion, they will give my daughter to the snake god. We only have a couple of days to find and kill the snake."

I needed to get to work.

We set up camp, and the men knew exactly what to do. I was impressed by their professionalism.

Chase came over to me with a cup of coffee. *Is it just me—or does coffee play a major role in my life and my dreams?* He said, "Can I help?"

I said, "No."

We looked at each other and smiled. There was definitely a spark when we looked at each other.

I said, "What do you see?"

He said, "I see a woman I want to kiss." He grabbed me and kissed me.

I pulled back and slapped him across the face. I was shocked by his boldness.

He said, "You didn't like my kiss?"

I said, "I like a kiss when I'm prepared."

He said, "I'm sorry. You are too irresistible. I couldn't help myself."

You are rude, sarcastic, and bold, but it was a good kiss.

The sun was going down, and the sky was beautiful. There was a cool breeze coming in, and the campfire was just what we needed to warm ourselves up. The moon was full, and it lit up the night. It seemed like it should be scary outside the cave with a huge snake inside, but it wasn't. It was peaceful and serene. I loved the perfect weather there: warm with no humidity during the day, cool and breezy at night.

Chase was by my side almost the whole time. I didn't mind. It was comforting to have him by my side. We got up early the next day. I had a tool belt around my waist. It had a place for my trowel, flashlight, and knives. I had rope wrapped around my chest. *I love being prepared.*

We took pictures of the rounded area outside the cave and the cave itself. The detail of the carvings was very intricate. The workmanship was incredible. The big question was who would lead us through the cave.

Nigel said, "I will lead."

Nobody argued.

It was dark and cool inside the cave. I had envisioned one tunnel that would lead to a big area where we would find the treasure. Much to our surprise, it was like a maze of tunnels. It seemed like forever, but we came to a cliff. The only way across was on a rope bridge. We crossed one person at a time. We could not see how far down the drop was because it was dark. Someone dropped a coin into the darkness, but we heard nothing. *Whoever built this bridge had nerves of steel!*

It was a long way across. Nigel assured us that it was sturdy as he went across. I followed behind him, and Chase was right behind me. *It's not my imagination. The man is stalking me. Okay, that's a little dramatic, but he is always by my side.*

I lost my step, and I leaned over to one side. The rope didn't give me the balance I needed, and I thought I was falling. My heart dropped. I got on my knees and held the rope.

Chase grabbed me, steadied me, and assisted me across the bridge. I had never been so frightened. I really thought I was falling over. I felt like I was on a roller coaster, and my heart was in my stomach.

When we reached the other side, I had to sit for a minute. I was feeling nauseous, but Chase never left my side.

One of the guys said, "This reminds me of the volcano incident."

I closed my eyes and fell asleep.

I woke up in my bed at home. I heard my daughter and son laughing I said, "What are you guys doing?"

They said, "We're coming." When they appeared in my room, both of them were holding a cup of coffee.

My daughter said, "Dad left early. We decided to bring you your coffee this morning to say thank you for a great weekend. We want to go away again soon."

My son said, "We want to go white-water rafting."

They started jumping up and down about the thought of going away again. Everybody seemed to be in such a good mood; even I felt happier. It really was a terrific weekend.

I was in a good mood, and I decided to cook steaks on the grill for dinner.

It was sunset when my husband came home. He said, "I thought I smelled something cooking on the grill. Let me take that fork. I'm the grill person around here."

I was more than happy to hand it over. The kids were swimming in the pool. Once again, everything seemed perfect. Since the weather was so nice, we decided to eat on the patio. Eating together as a family seems like a simple thing to do, but in everyday life, it's not so simple. My husband was working overtime, and the kids had crazy schedules. We didn't have time to sit down as a family that often. It was nice to have a conversation with the kids and my husband.

I said, "We need a new grill. This one is on its last legs."

To my surprise, my husband said, "Go buy a new one."

It really was a beautiful evening. The kids even cleaned up the dishes.

I was getting ready for bed when my husband pulled me toward him. He wanted to make love, and I willingly submitted. *I can't wait to get back to the cave to see what happens next.*

I fell asleep soon after our lovemaking.

When I woke up, Chase asked what passageway we should take. I could hear drums in the distance.

Nigel looked even more serious than usual. He said, "We don't have a lot of time. We must move on."

Chase grabbed my hand to help me up, and it felt so good that I didn't let go.

I asked him where he got the rope that was hanging around his shoulder.

He said that one of the guys had given it to him.

We heard a horrific hissing noise from the direction we were headed.

Nigel said, "It's the snake. He hears the sound of the drums."

Chills went down my spine as we headed in the direction of that horrible hissing sound. It seemed like we were in the cave for days. It was dark and cold as we moved deeper into the cavern. Going through tunnels and crossing antiquated bridges without proper lighting was difficult. A passageway led us to another bridge made of stone and wood planks. The planks were old and worn, but it was easy to get across.

Jake went first, and one of the planks came loose and fell down into the darkness. We didn't hear a sound as it fell.

Chase's muscles bulged through his T-shirt as he reached out to help Jake. I looked at Chase and thought, *I feel so safe with you.* I must have said it out loud because Chase looked at me with a huge grin.

We both giggled.

Everyone made it over the bridge. We got to a narrow tunnel, and it did not look like any of us could fit. We had to walk sideways to get through.

The drums got louder, and the hissing was closer. Everything seemed to be caving in on us. We came to an open area and saw rays of light through cracks in the cave. Everything in the cavern was glistening.

In the center of the cavern, there was a huge sculpted rock, which was shaped like an umbrella, and it had a ladder to the top. It was about twenty feet high. There was writing on the wall.

Nigel explained how the chiefs wrote messages for the gods. Their history was all over the cavern.

Jake and the guys were examining the artifacts to check their authenticity.

Chase and I inspected the beauty and workmanship the snake statue. The statue was a man with a turban and a python wrapped around him. The man was carved into the stone, and the snake was solid gold with rubies and diamonds as the eyes. We had never seen anything like it before. It looked like the snake had imprisoned the helpless man. It sent chills down my spine. It made me sad to see the man overpowered by the snake. Chase and I stepped back to look at the whole picture. There was a lot to take in.

Jake said, "Let me get a closer look at this statue. Any snakes at home?"

All hell broke loose. The hissing of the snake was loud and present, and then the glow of torches lit up the tunnels. *The natives are here.* I turned to Chase, but he was gone.

From out of nowhere, Chase swung down on a long rope, swooped me up, and brought me to safety.

The natives came into the cavern. Nigel's daughter was in the center of the group. They had an elaborate array of fruit and vegetable platters to please the gods. I couldn't believe what I was seeing. *Is this really happening? No. It's a dream.*

The natives were bowing to the statue like it was a real god.

A huge python appeared from the gold statue and slowly worked its way out of the statue.

Chase pulled out his gun and blasted the snake right between its eyes.

The natives started going crazy. Everyone was looking at the snake, bowing, and sobbing.

I quickly climbed up the ladder and stepped on top of the umbrella part of the rock. I picked up my trowel, wedged it into the stone, hooked my rope around it, swung down on the rope, and grabbed the girl. There was so much disarray that no one was paying attention to the girl. She almost slipped out of my hands. I struggled to get her to a safe place where we could hide out until the others could get to us.

Chase was watching in amazement at what I did. While I stayed with the girl, he got everyone together. We escaped through one of the tunnels, and Nigel showed us a place where we could rest. He and his daughter cried as they hugged each other. It was good to see them reunited, and it took away any doubts I had about this expedition. I knew we had done the right thing.

"Dynamite is the only way out of this cave," Jake said. "We have to move fast if we are going to do this. We don't have a choice. This is our only way out."

I said, "What about the snake statue, the treasure, and all the artifacts in the cavern? What about the history of these people?"

"We can't," he said. "This is our only chance to get out of here alive."

As an archeologist, I had to try to preserve this sacred ground.

Chase said, "Let's blow up the tunnels to hold the natives back while we escape. That won't destroy the cavern. We gathered as much information as we could for our research, and we have to make a decision. Now."

I tried to think things through. I closed my eyes for a split second, and when I opened them, I was in my bed at home. *I have to get back to my dream to tell them to blow up the tunnels and not the cavern.*

I heard the kids yelling outside by the pool. I heard my husband saying, "Knock it off, you guys!" I looked out the window, and my husband was cooking on our new grill. *What day is it? I must be losing track of the days. I cannot believe it is the weekend already. Time seems to be flying by.*

I put on my robe and went down to the patio to see what everyone was doing.

My husband asked if I had a good night's sleep. He said I was restless all night.

It was a huge snake. You bet I was restless.

It was an unusually beautiful morning, and my husband was using the new grill. It had gas burners, a rotisserie, and it even had built-in lights for grilling at nighttime. He was making eggs and French toast on the griddle. We spent a lovely morning on the patio.

I went shopping that afternoon, and my husband went to the office. He had to take a client to dinner, and we would have to eat without him.

This works out fine for me because I can get back to my dream! I got the kids takeout, and I nibbled on leftovers before bed.

I woke up, and Chase was holding me. We were still in the tunnel.

I said, "What is going on?"

He said, "We are trying to figure out what to do."

I said, "Blowing up the tunnels is the best way to go."

He and the guys quickly set up the dynamite, and we headed out of the cave.

It was good to see the sunlight. It felt like we were in that cave forever. They pulled the detonator as we all ran away from the cave.

Chase actually threw himself over me to protect me from any debris. Everyone was pushed to the ground from the force of the blast.

Once everything was calm, we quickly started back toward the plane. Stopping only once for water, we made it to the plane before sundown.

Nigel thanked us for saving his daughter and apologized for not being honest about the expedition.

Jake said, "We got pictures."

Chase turned to me and said, "I got you a little something." He pulled out a gold statue embedded with rubies and diamonds. It was a miniature version of the snake god statue. I just looked at him and gave him the biggest kiss. This time, he was the one who didn't let go.

Nigel decided to leave with us. He felt that he and his daughter would never be safe on the island.

The guys loaded the plane. I sat down and leaned against a tree.

Chase brought over a cup of coffee for me. He sat down beside me, and we leaned on each other. It was very romantic.

All of a sudden, we heard the natives in the distance.

"They're coming," Nigel shouted.

Everyone loaded the plane.

Chase started the engine, and we flew out of there. An hour into the flight, Chase came out of the cockpit.

I looked at him with a startled look.

He said, "It's on autopilot. I just came out for some coffee."

"I'm going to miss your sarcasm." *I wonder if we will ever see each other again.*

He looked me in the eyes and said, "I know we will—and who knows, maybe we'll come back to the island and search for the treasure again." He leaned down and gently kissed me.

I woke up in my bed. The moisture on the window told me it might rain. I had a lot of stuff to do around the house, but I just wanted to stay in bed. I was wondering where my coffee was, and then I realized my husband had to leave early for a client. *He has been so busy. I know he's making money for the family. He wants to go on a cruise, and he is working overtime to earn extra money. It is funny that Chase and I never made love. I will never know how it would have been with him, being one with him. I imagine he would be a beautiful, caring, and tender lover. I wonder if he will ever be in my dreams again. I guess I will find out.*

I started thinking about my husband. I realized that it was Sunday. *What client would Michael have on a Sunday morning? Sunday is our day to rest and enjoy each other. Clients on Saturday and Sunday? Is he cheating on me? Have I been so blind to think he has been working all this time? No. That is out of the question. He loves me. He would never cheat on me.*

I went to the kitchen, and the kids were getting ready to go to a baseball game at school. "Love you," they yelled as they walked out the door.

When my husband got home that afternoon, I said, "Where have you been all day?"

"My client flew in for the weekend, and this was the only time he could meet with me. I'm making big money, honey, and if I make a good impression with this guy, it could open a lot of doors. I hope you don't mind, but I invited him over for dinner. I can't wait for you to meet him. He's very interesting. He's a self-made millionaire. He has hotels all over the country, and he's a down-to-earth guy. You would never know he's a successful hotelier."

We were a little tired and napped before dinner. Michael went to our bedroom, and I went to the sofa. I did not think I would fall asleep, but I did.

The kids woke me up when they walked in the front door. *I am surprised I didn't have any dreams. I always have dreams. Oh, well. Maybe I will dream tonight.*

We decided to cook lamb chops on the grill. The sun was setting when his client arrived. We had a very enjoyable evening, and Michael's client told us stories of his earlier years and how he started in the hotel business. He was very interesting. The kids even got a kick out of his stories.

At one point, my husband looked at me and said, "You look very pretty tonight."

I said, "Thank you, honey. You are looking pretty good yourself."

By the end of the evening, we were tired. We could not wait to go to bed. It had been a long weekend.

When I went to sleep, I was surprised when I found myself getting off the jet. I just wanted to get home, take a shower, and lie down. Thoughts of Chase kept going through my mind. I thought that dream was over. I fell asleep thinking about him, and when I woke up, I was still in my dream.

I got up and started getting myself together. I had a big meeting with the board. The people who fund the excursions always want to know firsthand what went on and what we found. The meeting was going well. I had to explain about Nigel and his daughter. They were surprised to hear about the ritual and wanted to know every detail.

I showed them the pictures so they could see exactly what the cave looked like. As I was showing the pictures, I looked out the window and saw Chase. He was wearing a straw hat. He looked at me and winked.

I said, "Just a moment. I see the pilot who took us on this expedition. You will definitely want to talk to him. I ran out of the room and called for him. I told him what I was doing, and he was more than willing to come in and talk with the board.

When Chase came into the room, I introduced him to everyone. "He is such a great explorer, and he helped get us out of there alive. I have one more thing to show you." I pulled out the statue, and they gasped at its beauty.

At the end of the meeting, they congratulated us on a job well done.

I think the statue saved the day.

As we were leaving, Chase said, "How about going for a nice steak dinner?"

I looked at him, and said, "Like a date?"

He said, "Yes, like a date."

I knew I had steaks in the freezer at home, and I suggested grilling steaks at my house.

He said, "All right. That sounds like a great idea."

When the steaks were thawed and ready to go, Chase rang the doorbell; it was perfect timing. I poured him a glass of wine and threw the steaks on the grill. He got a kick out of looking at all the artifacts around my house.

He came out to the grill and said, "Let me flip those steaks."

We had a very romantic dinner. He told me how he became a pilot, and I told him how I became an archeologist.

He said, "Not only are you a great explorer—you're a great cook too." He grabbed me and kissed me. He had the sweetest-tasting lips, and I could see right through his eyes. He kissed my neck, my ears, and my lips over and over; he was so perfect. I felt like a wet noodle in his arms. I could not believe how romantic he was. He picked me up and walked me to the bed. He and I had a connection like magnets.

He said, "I never want to let you go."

We made love. I had never felt so much love toward anyone in my life. I devoured every kiss and every touch. I had never felt so nourished.

He whispered, "I'll always be yours."

We fell asleep in each other's arms.

CHAPTER 8

JP

I woke up and wanted to start my day. I had big plans to clean the garage. I like to clean it out every couple of months. It constantly gathers junk. I don't even know where it comes from. *First, where is my coffee?*

My husband left early again. *I will have to get it myself.* I always feel so accomplished when I clean the garage or organize a closet in the house. It just feels good to get something done and to have something to show for the work I have done. As a stay-at-home mom, I do not always feel like I'm getting things done.

When I finally got the garage cleaned, I had filled four fifty-five-gallon lawn bags.

I think I will order takeout tonight. Maybe I'll order ribs. They have a special tonight at the rib shack around the corner. Yeah, that sounds good. I do not think Michael will mind, and I know the kids will not mind. Okay, it's a plan!

I love when I come up with good ideas. I just want to have dinner, take a bubble bath, and get to bed. It had been a long day. Michael and the kids were happy to have ribs; I think it was a pleasant surprise for them. Michael said that his client enjoyed our family and would never turn down an invitation to come over when he is in town. I thought that was a nice compliment.

We were all tired. It wasn't a surprise that we fell asleep as soon as our heads hit the pillows.

I found myself in a bland office building. I looked down at my outfit, and I was wearing a gray skirt suit. I looked pretty boring too. I took a look in a mirror. My hair was in a tight bun, and my face was as white as a ghost. *Lovely*, I thought to myself, but there was one good thing. The figure-friendly suit looked good. At least I had that going for me because the rest of the look is a little scary.

As I walked through the office, I noticed the secretaries were very attentive toward me. They said hello and were very respectful as I walked by. I got to my office and sat at my desk. I found an envelope addressed to Katerina Arman. *I wonder what I do.*

A handsome man in a gray suit walked into my office. *Maybe this is a uniform because nobody dresses like this on purpose.* His suit fit him perfectly. He was built extremely well, and he looked good. He probably knew it too.

His expensive necktie showed me he had good taste. It had to be a Carmella.

I was about to smile and say hello, but he plopped paperwork down on my desk, turned around, and walked out without a word. I was a little shocked. *Who was that? I can't believe how rude that man was.*

My secretary walked in a few minutes later, and I was still in shock. I asked her who the man was.

She said, "Ms. Arman, that is Nicholas Myodor. He is your right-hand man. Are you feeling okay? Can I get you some water or something?"

"No. I'm fine. I am just having a moment. Maybe I'm working too much."

She said, "That's probably true. If you need me, I'll be right outside."

"Thank you, Nadine. I need you to call Nicholas to tell him I need to talk to him about this paperwork he just plopped on my desk."

"Okay," she said. "I am going to be very honest with you because you always tell me to be honest and frank. I must remind you that he has an attitude because you are his boss, and he thinks you are a snob."

I said, "Really? Thanks for filling me in."

"No problem. I'm right outside your office if you need me for anything."

"Just Nicholas. Thank you, Nadine."

A snob. I guess I'll just have to show him that I'm a very nice person. I'll show him that I'm very nice—and I say hello to people. I'm not rude like him.

Nicholas came into my office a few minutes later.

I said, "Are you ready to go?"

He replied, "Yes, I'll get the car."

I told him I would be down in a minute. I had to make a quick phone call. He nodded and walked out the door.

He was waiting outside the office in a black four-door sedan. I got in and we left. We had a long ride ahead of us. The man we were investigating had an office in the country. I had to review the file on the way.

Nicholas did not say one word to me; in fact, it felt very chilly for a hot summer day. His dislike toward me was obvious.

Cattle were crossing the road as we came around a bend. Nicholas slammed on the brakes. I was thrust forward, and his arm came up to hold me back. He was very strong, and his arm did not waver from the force of my body hitting it. I was in shock that I wasn't wearing a seat belt—and because he saved me from going through the windshield.

I looked at Nicholas and said, "Thank you."

He said, "You're welcome."

I said, "Are you prepared for the meeting?"

He said, "Yes, I'm prepared." He moved his jacket so I could see the revolver tucked in his belt.

I said, "Okay, let me do the talking."

He said, "You always do." We looked at each other with little smirks and continued talking.

"How did you choose this profession?" I asked.

He said, "You don't choose. They choose you."

That's right. I was chosen for this position. I must be very smart because I'm the boss. That's why everyone in the office is so attentive toward me.

We arrived at Ivan Kerig's office, and the receptionist had us wait in the lobby. I tapped a pen on the top of the file.

Nicholas said, "Can you calm down, woman?"

"Don't call me *woman*," I snapped. "Let's not forget I'm your boss—and I don't like being spoken to with such disdain."

Waiting is not one of my virtues.

He turned away, and then he smiled at me. I felt happy to have him smile at me.

We were shown to the conference room and told that Mr. Kerig would be right with us.

A few minutes later, this fairly good-looking, middle-aged man walked into the conference room and said, "Hello, I'm Ivan Kerig. An emergency has come up. Can you meet me tonight for cocktails."

Nicholas and I looked at each other. I was upset, but I had to act like it was not a problem. *Whatever is convenient for him. If I don't get this interview, I'll be sent to Siberia.*

Ivan Kerig thought we were interviewing him about his business. To my knowledge, he had no idea that he was being investigated for espionage. We decided that we would meet him for cocktails.

On the ride home, I told Nicholas that I would drop him off at home and pick him up later since he lived closer to where we were meeting Kerig. I could tell my thoughtfulness surprised him.

I went home and took a hot shower. I was admiring my body. I really had an awesome body. *I think this is my favorite part of the dream so far, maybe not. Nicholas is pretty interesting.*

I looked for something to wear. All I could find were more gray suits in my closet. *This has got to be a uniform. There is no way anyone would dress like this on purpose.*

In the back of the closet, I found a couple of dresses and a long gown. I picked the cutest dress I could find. *I'm so glad I don't have to wear that ugly suit, and I am going to wear my hair down. Enough of the Nurse Ratched look. Wearing my hair in such a tight bun gives me a headache. No wonder people think I'm uptight.*

It had been a long day, and I decided to take a nap before going out. When I woke up, I was in my bed. The smell of coffee shifted my thoughts to my real life. I realized I was starving.

The kids were home, and I made French toast the way my grandmother used to make it. My grandmother was a great cook; she could make anything out of nothing. Michael loved it when she came over because there would always be a feast when he got home. She was a little Italian lady and wore a housedress and apron.

"Madonna me," she would say, waving a wooden spoon in the air. "What am I gonna do with you kids? Madonna me!" It seems like another lifetime, but I have to do the same to my kids. I say "Madonna me. What's the matter with you!"

The kids looked at me like I'm weird, and I just smile. *They think I'm a little crazy, and outbursts like that just confirm their thoughts.*

After breakfast, I decided to relax around the pool. I deserved a "me" day.

My husband came home with a bouquet of flowers. He said, "These are for you."

"What's the occasion?" I asked.

Michael said, "We got the contract." I had not seen him so happy in a long time. He said, "Anywhere you want to go—a cruise, the mountains, name it. I want to celebrate, but can we do it tomorrow night? I'm exhausted from all the work I've been putting into this deal."

I said, "That sounds great, honey. Tomorrow night. It's a date."

We went to bed on the early side. I think Michael fell asleep before his head hit the pillow.

When I woke up in my apartment, I sat up and looked at the clock. It was almost time to leave. I got up and started to get ready. I found a beautiful box on top of the vanity. I opened it up, and it had the most exquisite jewelry. *If I have jewelry like this, I must go out.* I looked in the mirror. My face was still so white. I put on some makeup to add some life to me. I got dressed and looked in the mirror one more time. I thought I looked way better.

I called down to the doorman, and my car was waiting when I got downstairs. *I like this kind of living. I feel like I'm in a hotel. I could get used to this.*

I went to pick up Nicholas and thought about how cold he was. I hoped he would be nicer that evening. When I arrived at his house, it had started to rain. I blew the horn since I did not want to get wet. *I hope he does not think I am rude for not coming to the door.*

He came right out.

I said, "Boy, you are right on time."

He said, "I'm not going to make you wait."

I replied, "I'm not that way."

"What did you do?" he said with a smile. "You look great, woman."

"Don't call me *woman*."

"I know," he said. "I'm sorry."

I felt good that he thought I looked great, though.

The hotel was fancy, but I was dressed appropriately for the meeting. When we approached the table where Ivan was sitting, he stood up to greet us.

When we sat down, Ivan did not waste any time getting down to business. "What are you looking for?" he asked.

I looked at Nicholas, took a deep breath, and told him we had reason to believe he was committing espionage.

He said, "I don't know where you would get this information, but you have been misinformed. My country is everything to me, and I would never commit such a crime. This meeting is over."

I said, "Okay, but you can't leave the country until our investigation is over."

He looked at us, got up, and left.

I started to get up, but Nicholas grabbed my arm and said, "Let's stay and have a drink. Why waste a perfectly good evening?"

I looked into his eyes. He was starting to open up to me in the way I had hoped. "Yes, let's have a drink."

We had a few drinks and talked about our childhoods. He saw people get killed because they didn't adhere to the rules that had been implemented by our country. This left horrible scars of injustice in his mind. He said he would help someone in need even if it meant going against the rules. He asked if I would ever turn a blind eye to help others.

"I can't say that I would or wouldn't. I honestly don't know. What exactly are you talking about?"

Music started playing, which was good because it lightened the mood, and he asked if I would like to dance.

When we went to the dance floor, a slow song was playing. He held me close, and it made me feel safe. He held me so gently, and I loved it. I felt like he was holding me for the longest time. I didn't want him to let me go.

On our way home, he asked if there was anything I wanted him to do for tomorrow.

I said, "Yes, can you type this up for me and create a file."

He answered yes very arrogantly—which I thought was odd.

When I pulled up to his house, he took my hand and kissed me good night.

I went back to my apartment in a daze from his kiss. I went out on my balcony and looked up at the sky. *What is this dream all about? Nicholas is certainly not the dull man he portrays himself to be. I wonder what is going to happen.*

I wanted to take a shower before bed. In the shower, I thought about him kissing me. It sent chills all over my body. After a hot shower, I went to bed and fell right asleep.

I woke up and remembered I had promised to help my friend clean her mother's house. Her mother was handicapped and couldn't do it herself. I had a cup of coffee before she picked me up.

When I got in her car, my friend said, "You've got stars in your eyes. Sometimes they look distant, like you are somewhere else. What's going on?"

I said, "Nothing. Okay, okay. I haven't told you everything about my dreams."

We got to her mom's house and started cleaning. There was a lot to do, but telling her about my dreams made the time go by faster. I told her about Kane, Danielle, John, Christopher, and Jarred.

She was in shock. "My God, your dreams are like a motion picture or a miniseries. Wow, you have the best nightlife of anyone I know. I think John is my favorite. No, maybe Jarred. All I know is I want to dream like that."

Before we knew it, we were done. Her mother was very grateful, and we were pleased that we could help her.

I remembered that Michael and I were going to celebrate his new contract that night.

On the way home, I got a text from him. There were some last-minute complications that needed to be taken care of. Dinner would have to wait for another night. He texted, "Don't wait for me to have dinner. I'll grab a bite later. Sorry."

I couldn't have been happier. I just wanted to go home, take a hot bath, and get in bed. I let the kids order a pizza. They were thrilled.

When my husband arrived home, he made himself a scotch and watched the end of a basketball game. I had a headache, and I took a couple of aspirin before bed. I fell asleep and woke up in the morning.

I rushed to get dressed in that horrible polyester suit and put my hair in a tight bun. I looked in the mirror. *I look like a parole officer. This is not my style. Why do I dress like this? Oh well.*

I went to work, and I was smiling. My secretary came right in and said, "What is the good news?"

I looked at her and said, "What are you talking about?"

She said, "You're smiling. I thought something was going on."

"What? I can't smile? Is something wrong with smiling?"

"No. It's just that you don't."

"I don't what?"

"Nothing. Would you like a cup of coffee?"

"Yes, please. That would be nice."

After she left, Nicholas came in and dropped off the file.

I said, "Thank you."

He looked surprised. *What is with these people? Can't someone be nice?*

I asked how the research on Ivan was going.

He said, "It's a dead end. I don't think we are going to find anything."

"Well, you know we have to be very thorough. Keep looking. Oh, by the way, I received a memo. Apparently someone in our organization is a double agent."

He asked, "Who do you think it is?"

"I don't know, but I need you to keep your ears and eyes open, okay?"

He looked a little startled and said, "I'll certainly keep an eye out."

At the end of the day, he popped his head in the door to say good night.

I said, "Good night. Hey, how about having dinner with me tonight?"

"That sounds great. I would love it."

"Great. I'll cook at my flat … seven o'clock?"

"Sounds good. I'll see you tonight."

I stopped by the market for fresh fish and vegetables. I was feeling romantic and got a bottle of wine too. *I think Nurse Ratched's going to let her hair down.* I got home, immediately changed into something more comfortable, and let my hair down. *That's better.*

I look absolutely hideous in that polyester uniform. The only good thing about the polyester is that everyone has to wear the same thing.

I was in the kitchen when the doorman called to let me know Nicholas had arrived. I told him he could send Nicholas right up.

"Something smells good," he said as he walked in.

I said, "I only hope it tastes as good as it smells."

He said, "Well, I only hope it tastes as good as you look."

The sparks were flying between us. I told him dinner would be ready in about twenty minutes.

We went to the balcony with the bottle of wine and talked. When he poured the wine, I couldn't help but notice how confident and suave he was.

I said, "I am from the mountainside, and my family was not rich by any stretch. When the agency profiled me for the position, they made it very attractive for me—and my family. I work for the agency, and they provide for my mother and father. I was groomed for this position.

"The agency began to train me for this position when I was still in school. As soon as school was over, I was ready to go to work. They wasted no time. Time is money. They are probably grooming someone for my position as we speak. There is pressure to keep everyone happy—the agency and my parents. That is probably why I always look so uptight. I do not live a life of happiness. I live to make others happy."

Nicholas talked about his childhood a little bit, but he was more interested about the double agent. "Who do you think it could be?"

I said, "I don't know, but I need your help." He noticed my glass was empty and asked if I would like another glass. I was a bit tipsy from the first glass, but I still said yes.

As he poured the wine, our hands touched. I could feel the energy flowing between us. Just then, it started to rain. We grabbed the wine and our goblets and went inside. My thin silk shirt was soaked. I was cold from the air-conditioning in my apartment. My nipples were protruding through my shirt.

He grabbed my robe and draped it around me to warm me up. With the sexiest voice, he said, "Why don't you change out of those wet clothes?"

I looked at him and said, "That's probably a good idea." As I left to change, he pulled me to him so gently. I wasn't offended because he had a gentle way about himself. I was glad he pulled me to him. As I wrapped my arms around him, my robe fell to the floor.

He helped me take my shirt off as we walked over to my bed. "I can't do this."

I asked, "What's wrong?"

He said, "This is not the way I want to be with you. Excuse me. I want you to have a clear head."

I smiled and said, "I want you to take advantage of me. I'm throwing myself at you. Trust me. It is okay."

We moved to the bed. His body was so close to mine. We were like two pieces of a puzzle that perfectly matched. He was on top of me, and I could feel how hard he was. I was pleased to know he was as turned on as I was.

He took his time. He was in no rush. He was kissing me all over my neck and my body; with my breasts exposed, he had full access. He was turning me on so much. I wanted to rip my pants off, but I waited. I wanted to see how he would handle himself. He took his time. He slowly unbuttoned my pants and slowly slipped them off. I was on another planet. I didn't even notice him taking his shirt off. His skin was soft and smooth. I touched every part of his body, soaking him up.

Our energy is powerful. I never knew it could be like this. I always wondered, but I knew there was no time for love or romance in my life—just work.

I felt like I was going to explode. I wanted him inside of me now. I did not know how to handle myself. I felt so out of control; it was like an insatiable taste for something, and I just couldn't get it fast enough. It was insane. I could only feel that way with someone I felt safe with, and I did feel safe with Nicholas. I knew he had the same appetite for me that I had for him. I felt relieved that I wasn't alone in my desperation. I knew he needed me just as much.

I had never been with anyone before. He was my first, and I was glad I waited because it was how I always imagined it would be. *I never want to let him go. He is everything I've ever wanted. He fills that deep, empty void I have been feeling my whole life.* We held each other tightly and fell asleep. The next thing I knew, I woke up.

I was thinking about how good it felt to be loved like that. It's not that my husband doesn't love me, but he doesn't put effort into our lovemaking like Nicholas. I think my husband loves me. It's just that there is something missing. I don't think my husband could ever give me the affection I need. Who is the double agent? Where is this dream going?

My husband brought me coffee and said, "Tonight is the night we are going to celebrate." He handed me some money and told me to go buy a new outfit.

Why do I want to dress up for a man who doesn't look at me like a woman even when I do dress up? I am so confused. I don't know what's going on in his mind. Maybe I'm just going through a midlife crisis or something. Maybe tomorrow I'll be back in love with him—and everything will be okay. I'm starting to get a headache. I don't want to think anymore.

I had my daughter to go shopping with me, and we both ended up getting new outfits. When we returned home, my daughter wanted to show her friend her new outfit.

I was starving and ate a sandwich by the pool. It was such a beautiful day, and the patio looked so inviting. I fell asleep on a lounge chair. I woke up when the front door slammed; my husband was home from work.

He was in a really good mood. He said, "I'm going to get dressed. We have reservations at seven."

Having a new outfit made me feel excited. It almost felt like when we were younger and going out on a date. We got ready, and I fixed his tie. We complimented each other on how we looked, and I thought, *Boy, that's a first.*

The restaurant had music and dancing, which I loved. We started with champagne, of course, followed by dinner, wine, and dancing. It was fun.

My husband said, "I want to make you happy. How can I make you happy?"

I was not ready for the conversation at all. I'd had had a few drinks. I was relaxed. I could not think. I said, "Michael, I've been drinking and dancing all night. I'm tired. Can we talk about this another night? Please?"

He said, "Okay, another night, but the night's not over yet."

I said, "Okay."

We ran into a couple of his partners and had a drink with them. It was a great evening. Everybody was in such a good mood.

After a while, the wine started getting to me. I looked at my husband and said, "Are you ready to go?"

He said, "Yes."

I smiled and said, "Good."

We got home and fell asleep.

When I woke up, it was morning. Nicholas was with me. We got up, and he rushed to leave. He still had to go home to get ready for work.

I called the doorman to pull his car up, kissed him good-bye, and said, "I'll see you at the office." It felt as though we were married. I rushed to get ready too. I put on my gray polyester uniform and left for work. I thought of Nicholas during the entire drive.

When I got to the office, I was rushing, but I did notice people whispering. My secretary told me that the chief officer of internal affairs was waiting for me in my office along with a few other high-ranking officers. I said, "Thank you. I'll have to see what they want."

When I walked in, they stood up and saluted. I saluted back. We all sat down, and they explained that they had narrowed it down to a couple of people and they thought they might know exactly who the double agent was. They wouldn't tell me, but they did ask questions about Nicholas. *Nicholas is our double agent?* I asked if Nicholas was the double agent, but they only said that they wanted me to find out more information.

While they were talking, I thought about how cruel they were. *I hope they don't think I'm a part of some sort of conspiracy. The KGB is responsible for silencing or eliminating dissidents. Would they go after my parents if they suspected I was a part of anything just to prove a point?*

Nicholas came into my office to drop off a file, but the officers didn't even give him a glance. They acted like he was invisible. He looked at me, put the file on my desk, and walked out.

After they left, I wasn't sure what to say or do.

Nicholas came in and said, "What's going on? It looked pretty serious in your office."

I said, "Nicholas, they think you are a double agent. I'm supposed to get information from you. I can't talk here. Let's have dinner tonight. I'm going to leave. I have a headache. We'll talk tonight."

I told my secretary to reschedule any appointments and went home at lunchtime. I was extremely upset about the meeting with internal affairs. I could not get myself together. I was thinking about Nicholas and my parents and how I opened myself up to Nicholas. *What am I going to do if he really is a double agent? How is that going to affect me? How is that going to affect my family? How is that going to affect my relationship with Nicholas?*

After a hot shower, I could smell the scent of Nicholas on my pillow. I just wanted to go to sleep. My mind was racing with all kinds of thoughts. Finally, I fell asleep.

I woke up in my bed and smelled fresh-brewed coffee. My husband had taken his shower already and was getting dressed. When I walked by him, he slapped me on the butt.

I said, "Hey, what was that for?"

He said, "We didn't do anything last night. You looked so beautiful last night. What's on your agenda today?"

I said, "I'm having lunch with a friend."

He said, "Maybe I can meet you."

"That would be great, but we are having lunch downtown."

"Oh, I just remembered I have a meeting at one o'clock. I won't have enough time to get back to the office. Maybe another day. How are you going to take the kids to the beach today if you are having lunch downtown?"

I said, "Honey, they are old enough to drop off. They are not little anymore."

He said, "Why am I asking? You know how to handle your own schedule."

"Thank you," I said.

He said, "Have fun today."

I felt like going back to sleep for a bit. I asked him to call me in an hour to make sure I was up.

When I woke up, I was in my apartment. All I could think is, *how could he be a double agent?* I was feeling nauseous. I went out to my balcony to get some fresh air. *What will I do if Nicholas is a double agent?*

When I looked at the time, it was getting late, and he would be arriving soon. *What am I going to cook?* I looked in my freezer and found some salmon fillets. *I have an old family recipe for salmon with sherry that will be perfect.* I got everything ready for the oven, and I went in my bedroom to freshen up.

About ten minutes later, the phone rang. It was the doorman announcing Nicholas.

I said, "Thank you. Send him up, please."

I opened the door as he was getting ready to knock. I said, "That was fast."

He said, "Something smells good."

I said, "Oh, it's an old family recipe. I hope you like it."

I shut the door behind him. We looked at each other for a minute. I couldn't hold back. "Nicholas, I need to know if you are the double agent."

His eyes got wide as he looked at me, and I knew immediately. "I don't call myself a double agent, Katerina," he said. "I help people find a better life."

I said, "Oh my God. It's true. You are."

"No. It's not that way, Katerina. I'm telling you I help people. You have to believe me."

"Nicholas, I want to believe you, but I also know what the KGB is capable of doing to people like us—and they know about us. They want me to get information out of you."

"Katerina, if you come to one of my meetings, you will understand everything. I tell people to fight for what they feel is right. These people are forced to work like slaves and have nothing. Their lives will never get better if they don't stand up for themselves."

"I can't go to your meeting. They will find out. It's not about me so much; it's about my family. They will harm my family."

"I promise they will never find out."

I felt better after talking to him, but I still was in fear for my life. He was a good person, a compassionate person, and I trusted him. I told him to get a gun because they were watching him, and they would go after him.

We sat on the couch, and he held me for the longest time. When I reached up to dim the lights, I caught his eyes. They had so much love in them. As he looked at me, my heart melted. I was so aroused from just that look. I'd never felt that kind of love before. When he looked at me, I had such an intense feeling. Electricity was running through my body. I felt like he was a part of me. He giggled.

I said, "What are you laughing at?"

He said, "I never imagined having such strong feelings toward you. I used to think you were a snob. I never would have thought of you and me together, but no other woman has ever affected me this way."

The radio was playing slow music. He asked me to dance, and we kissed passionately.

He said, "I need you so much."

I said, "I need you too."

He lifted me up, brought me to my bedroom, and started undressing me. We made love, and he was warm, tender, and loving. All secrets were on the table. Nobody had anything to hide. We were like two lost souls who had just discovered each other for the first time. He was everything I ever wanted and needed, and I wasn't ever going to let him go.

I whispered, "I'll be here to help you and protect you."

He whispered, "I'll be here to protect you too."

After we made love, we fell asleep in each other's arms. That time, I wasn't letting go. I woke up feeling so peaceful. *Shucks, I didn't want to wake up.*

I looked at the clock. It was ten o'clock. I had to get up if I was going to get the kids to the beach and meet my friend for lunch. I yelled to the kids, "Are you ready to go?"

My daughter came into my bedroom with her new bathing suit on. She loved it and couldn't wait for her friends to see it.

I couldn't wait to get back to Nicholas. I couldn't help but wonder if there were someone in real life like him. Nicholas made me feel like the most important person.

Michael called and asked about the kids, the beach, and lunch. I think he really wanted to come, but he had a meeting.

I got the kids to the beach and met my friend for a nice lunch. We caught up on everything.

When I got to the beach, a bunch of teenagers were dancing having a good time.

My daughter walked up to my car and begged me to let her stay longer.

I said, "We have to go, honey. It's getting late."

She was upset, but she knew it was time to go. When I got home, there was a package on the table. *Who could have put the package there? Nobody has been home.*

I called my husband to ask if the mysterious package was his. I said, "You had better get home. I feel like someone came into the house while I was away."

He started laughing and said, "Rayne, it is okay. I put the package there. I thought it would be a nice surprise for you when you got home today. The guy who we just signed the big business deal with sent our family gifts. That, my dear, is yours."

I went over to the table and opened the gift. I was excited. I loved gifts. Much to my surprise, it was a beautiful and expensive silk negligee from Italy. Michael was still on the phone while I opened it. I said, "Michael, why would he buy me a silk negligee? Isn't that personal?"

He said, "It was my idea. He asked me what you would like, and I told him what I thought you would like. You can model it for me when I get home."

I'm not modeling, but it is gorgeous. I said, "I'm tired."

He said, "You are always tired. Maybe you need to take some vitamins."

Maybe you're right.

I made dinner for Michael and left it on the stove for him. I got myself a cup of coffee, went out to the pool, and fell asleep on the lounge.

This time, I woke up to my husband saying something smelled good. My daughter was with her girlfriend in her bedroom.

I said, "I made dinner for you. It's on the stove."

He said, "You do look tired. Why don't you lie down?"

I said, "I think I will." Before I went to sleep, I told my husband I'd model the negligee the next day.

When I woke up, Nicholas was still holding me. I think I wanted to be with Nicholas. That's why I had been so tired. I felt comfortable and protected with his arms wrapped around me. I didn't want to get up, but I did.

He said, "Where are you going?"

I said, "To get some coffee. Would you like some?"

"Yes, that would be great. Thanks."

When I came back into the room, he was dressed and ready to go.

I just looked at him with a puzzled expression.

He said, "I'm going to leave work early today. Do I have your permission?"

"Yes, what's going on?"

"There is a meeting tonight. Do you want to go?"

"I'll think about it. I'll call you. In case they are listening to our conversation, I will simply say let's meet for lunch tomorrow. That will let you know yes."

The KGB knew I was picking his brain. I thought it would be safe for us to have lunch. Before he left, I grabbed his hand and told him I was going to the meeting.

He said, "Good. Meet me on Ridge Road at eight o'clock tonight. You will see my car. We can go together." He started to kiss me.

I said, "We can't let everyone know."

We met at Ridge Road. When I got into his car, he told me they had been asking questions. "They took two people in for questioning, and we are afraid they are going to take them to prison. The KGB is very good at twisting the truth."

When we got to the meeting, I was surprised by how many people were in attendance. They were good people. Nicholas introduced me to everyone and explained that I was not one of them. He said I could be trusted. He said, "The KGB is getting closer. They have recently questioned two of our people, and it appears they will be coming after them soon. We have to get them out of the country before the KGB has a chance to come back for them."

I realized that these people were just like my mother and father.

After the meeting, everyone slowly went in different directions so they wouldn't draw attention. I sat in Nicholas's car for a while. He squeezed my hand. *I can't believe how much touching my hand excites me.*

He said, "I'm going to take you back to your car now. I'm not going to see you tonight, but I'm going to need your help getting these people out of the country."

"Whatever I can do to help, I will do."

When I got home, I collapsed on my bed and fell asleep.

I woke up in my bed, and loud music startled me. I yelled, "Turn the music down."

My husband walked in with some coffee and toast. "Thank God they listen to you because they certainly didn't listen to me. I heard that most of the morning."

I had slept pretty late.

My husband left for the day, and the kids were going swimming. My husband had said something about them inviting friends over. In any case, I needed to get up. I put on some sweatpants, but then I changed my mind and put on shorts. It was hot outside. I went out to the pool and asked them what they were doing. "Do you want to go to lunch today?"

"Could you get lunch and bring it home for us?"

I went into the house and thought about Nicholas. *I really like him. I admire someone who helps people the way he does. I wonder if*

I will ever meet someone in my real life like him. What am I saying? I have to get myself together. I'm living in two worlds. I couldn't help but wonder what I would do if I met someone like Nicholas in real life.

I ran into an old friend at the grocery store. I hadn't seen in months. He invited my husband and I out to dinner. I told him it sounded great, and I'd call to set it up.

I brought back fried chicken, cold cuts, chips, and soda for the kids. The kids were being good, and they were very respectful. I told them lunch was in the kitchen when they were ready. They wanted to eat outside, and I told them I wouldn't have it any other way. I also got some steaks to grill for dinner.

I was thinking of my dream, and I couldn't stop wondering what was going to happen to those people. Would they get out of the country? The day went by so fast, and when my husband got home, it almost felt like he had just left.

With a big grin, he said, "I hope you saved some energy to model the lingerie tonight."

I didn't forget. I knew we were going to make love if I put on the lingerie. Much to my surprise, he was very gentle and caring as he made love to me.

I finally went to sleep and woke to the phone ringing.

Nicholas said, "You have to leave your apartment now. The KGB is on its way to see you. Get out now!"

Panic came over me. *How did they find out so quickly?* I pulled on some pants and sneakers. I didn't know what was going to happen, and I wanted to be ready for anything. I called the doorman for my car. When I got in my car, I noticed the KGB car pull up after me.

I could see the doorman pointing to my car as I pulled away.

Nicholas called and said, "We have the couple they were questioning. They are safe."

"The KGB is following me. What do you want me to do?"

"Just meet me at the warehouses near Ridge Road."

When I pulled up to the warehouses, Nicholas was waiting. I was so nervous; all I could think about was my mother and father.

The KGB car turned into the parking lot.

Nicholas said, "Listen to me. You need to go into the warehouse. Everyone's waiting there. I have to take care of these men. I can't allow them to find out about our organization. There are too many lives at risk."

"Nicholas, don't get hurt. I've fallen in love with you, and I don't want to be without you."

"Katerina, you have to go." I was surprised at how serious his voice had gotten.

I haven't seen this side of him before.

He said, "I'll come get you when I'm done."

I was fearful that he would get killed. I met the people in the warehouse and introduced myself. They already knew who I was.

After a while, we heard shooting. My worst fears were coming true. *What am I going to do without him? I don't think I can live without him.* I looked at the couple who had to leave the country and their children. *How can I possibly feel bad for myself? These people could lose everything, and I'm feeling sorry for myself. I have to get myself together.*

We heard someone enter the warehouse, but we did not know what would come next.

Nicholas came in and said, "We have to get rid of their car, the bodies, and any evidence that they were here." He introduced me to everyone, including the kids of the couple they wanted to arrest.

I said, "Nicholas, they were going to take the parents away from their children. That is why I have to help these people. The KGB just destroys and takes what it wants for its own benefit. I have to fight for these people. I want to be with you, Nicholas. I believe in what you do. I want to be an agent for you. Let's get rid of the evidence—and then we will talk."

He looked at me with the sweetest smile and said, "Okay, boss. Whatever you say."

Nicholas told me to go back to my apartment and wait for his call. He needed to take care of the car and make it look like the men were the double agents the agency had been looking for. After he got rid of the bodies, he and some men parked the car at the airport and left evidence in the car that would incriminate the KGB agents. It would look like the double agents were trying to leave the country.

Nicholas called me a couple hours later to see if I was okay. He said, "Would you like some company? I'll bring dinner."

I jumped up and got in the shower. I put on the perfume he liked and some comfortable lounging clothes.

The doorman announced Nicholas, and he was at my door before I knew it.

I opened the door, and we held each other.

I said, "Do you know what they will do to us if we get caught? I will have to leave the country. My parents will have to leave too."

The radio announcer said they were looking for KGB agents who had tried to leave the country. They gave the description of the men that Nicholas had killed.

I said, "You have an angel looking over your shoulder. I can't believe this."

We laughed, had a glass of wine, and breathed a sigh of joy. Needless to say, we slept soundly, woke up, and went into the office. I got there before Nicholas because he had to go home and get fresh clothes.

When I got to the office, my secretary told me the KGB agents were waiting in my office. I didn't know what to think. *I thought we were safe. Why would they be in my office? Was it all a hoax? Are they here to arrest me?*

I started to panic again. I went into my office. They introduced themselves and apologized for accusing the wrong man. "Those men wanted to lead us to believe it was Nicholas. Katerina, we know how loyal you are to our country, and we wanted you to hear it from us first how sorry we are for any inconvenience."

Nicholas stuck his head in the door to make sure everything was all right. My secretary must have told him they were in my office. They stood up, introduced themselves to Nicholas, and apologized for the accusations.

Later that day, he got me in the supply closet and gave me the most passionate kiss. He said, "I want you to be with me forever." It was music to my ears because all that I wanted was to be with him.

I went home early to take a nap. With all the excitement, I needed to sleep. I fell asleep in my bed and woke up to the smell of coffee. I wondered if I would have any more dreams because Nicholas was truly all I wanted. I couldn't imagine wanting anyone else.

I suddenly realized that the dreams were telling me something about my life. They were telling me that my husband and I needed to make some serious changes in our relationship if we were going stay together. *I obviously need more excitement. I need more love. And I need more warmth. I know I love my husband, but it's not enough. I need so much more out of a relationship and so much more out of life. When I was young, I was a dreamer—but I let those dreams go.*

CHAPTER 9

❧

I woke up to the smell of coffee. *Why do I always wake up to the smell of coffee? Is it waking me up to more than I have realized?*

My husband brought me a cup and said, "Don't forget we are going out tonight. We are going to meet some new clients. They are a very wealthy family who own a vineyard. The gentleman who owns it likes to deal with people who have a healthy and happy family life. He feels it is fruitful to deal with people who have strong family values like he does."

Since it was several hours away, we were going to spend the night at a bed-and-breakfast near the vineyard. The kids made plans to spend the night at their friends' houses. I had packed an overnight bag for Michael, and the kids got themselves together. A perk of having teenagers is that they can pack for themselves.

I had a few hours before Michael got home to leave for the vineyard. I took a nap, and I woke up on a hill in a beautiful countryside. I was dressed like a maid. My dress was a simple white cotton dress with an apron. My hair was down, and a white cloth band held it back off my face. I saw a small farm in the distance with horses and cows. I wondered who lived there. I heard someone yelling, "Tyler Danielle?" *Who is he yelling for?* The view from where I sat was spectacular. I could see for miles, and the sky was the bluest blue. It was incredible. I didn't know where I was, but I was glad to be there. It was magnificent.

In the distance, I saw men in armored suits riding horses. *Men in armor? What is this dream about?*

The voice started getting closer. An older man with a goatee said, "Tyler Danielle, there you are. Have you done your chores yet? Mary is waiting in the kitchen for the milk."

I said, "I'll do it now, Father."

Do I know how to milk a cow? I've seen it on television but never in person. Much to my surprise, I knew exactly what to do.

I brought the milk to Mary when I was done. We all sat down and ate breakfast together like a family. My mother had died a few years earlier, and Mary lived a few miles away. My father had asked her to help with the household duties. She was a very pleasant lady, and she was good company for my father too.

My father asked what I was doing today.

I said, "I am going to sit on the hill and sing and play my mandolin."

He said, "Don't go too far today. There are some conflicts going on around the countryside. It might be dangerous to go off alone."

"That's why I saw those armored men in the distance this morning."

He said, "Maybe I'll come and sit with you for a while. I do love to listen to your voice. It reminds me of your mother. After I feed the animals, I'll come up."

"See you on the hill, Father."

"Thank you, Mary, for breakfast. It was wonderful."

When I got up the hill, I saw men across the lake. I started to daydream about my Prince Charming on a white horse. I pictured him lifting his helmet, revealing how beautiful he was, and looking into my eyes. His loving gaze would tell me he's mine, and he would take me away to our beautiful castle where we would live happily ever after. I loved to daydream about my Prince Charming. It made me feel alive and full of promise that he did exist. I hoped fairy tales came true.

My father rushed up the hill and said, "Tyler, we must hide you in the barn." He grabbed my hand and pulled me with him. "I just got word that the knights are rounding up young ladies to serve their squires while they are in training. Squires are the up-and-coming knights who show great promise in serving the king. In return for their hard work, they give them a young girl to wed who will serve them and their needs. Hurry. We must hide you. They are on their way."

I said, "Father, I wouldn't mind a knight taking me away."

He said, "It's not what you might think, darling. They are not going to treat you with the love and respect you deserve. Let's at least go back to the house. That way, you are out of sight." Although he tried to conceal his emotions, I could tell my father was nervous. I don't think he could handle losing me; he barely survived losing my mother. I think having me kept him alive.

When we got back to the house, Mary was baking my favorite bread. We were lucky to have her. She had a calm way of soothing any tension. She said she would teach me how to bake. It was the perfect afternoon to learn. I loved the smell of fresh bread baking; its aroma made our home feel warm and cozy.

That night, I heard knights ride by on horseback. I fell asleep dreaming of my prince.

I woke up to the smell of coffee. My husband must have been making me a cup for the ride. I said, "When did you get home?"

He said, "Just a few minutes ago. Are you ready to go?"

I said, "Yes. I just need to change my clothes."

We arrived at the vineyard at five o'clock, which was perfect because it gave us time to go to our room and freshen up before dinner.

The entrance to the vineyard was absolutely beautiful; it reminded me of a beautiful hotel we stayed at years ago called the La Quinta in Palm Springs. It was a Mediterranean-style home with bougainvillea cascading down from the second-floor balcony. Gorgeous French doors opened onto the first-floor patio.

A man in a white coat greeted us formally. He said that Mr. Catalfamo and his wife were waiting to have a drink with us before dinner. He told us our bed-and-breakfast was on the property, and he would be happy to escort us after we had drinks.

Their home was right out of a magazine. I couldn't stop looking around at everything. It was perfectly kept and decorated. Our home had more of a lived-in feeling, but this house looked like a model home. It was very old, but they maintained it well. *If I had a dream home, this would be it.*

All of sudden, I felt excited. *This is a home I could see myself living in.* I always get excited when I love something. *It isn't a man this time. It is a home.*

As soon as we walked in, Mr. Catalfamo opened a bottle of wine from the vineyard. Mrs. Catalfamo showed us around their home and told us the history of their family. I could tell they were very proud of their accomplishments.

Before dinner, we went to change our clothes. When they picked us up for dinner, they were in a limo. Everything they did was first class. I didn't expect to love it so much. The restaurant looked like an old home that had been transformed into a charming restaurant. I loved exclusive, discreet service. I could tell it was very expensive, and they treated us like we were the most important people to walk through their doors, probably because we were with the Catalfamos.

They couldn't have been more inviting. Everyone knew their names, and they gave all of us the royal treatment. He graciously announced that we could have anything we wanted on the menu. He looked like Santa Claus complete with a twinkle in his eye and white hair and beard.

I saw a waiter pass by with a gorgeous shrimp cocktail. They looked like lobster tails. I'd never seen them so big. When dinner arrived, silver domes covered the dishes. When everyone was served, the waiters removed the silver domes and said, "Voilà."

The dinner was superb. *I could get used to this. I can't remember enjoying myself so much. It is like everything I loved has been put right before me—almost everything.*

Mrs. Catalfamo announced that she had baked a boysenberry pie and would like us to join them at their home for some coffee and pie.

She must be quite the homemaker. I asked if she grew the boysenberries, and she laughed and said, "Yes, how did you know?"

Mr. Catalfamo boasted that she made the best boysenberry pie anywhere. After pie and coffee, which was the best pie I'd ever had, the chauffeur took us back to our room.

My husband asked if I'd brought the red negligee. I had. I took a shower when we got back. It felt so good to take a shower. I stayed in there for a while, just relaxing myself before having sex with my husband. *I feel so bad that I feel this way, but this isn't something that just happened overnight. This process has taken years to develop, and lack of communication and not sharing our feelings was the culprit. I literally shut myself down. I don't know how to open up to him. I don't know how to explain that I'm not happy. I haven't been happy for a long time.*

I got out of the shower and put on my negligee. I looked good.

Michael saw me and said, "I love you, and you look so beautiful. Can we make love tomorrow? I'm so full and tired. I could just go right to sleep."

Relief came over me. I said, "Not a problem. I'm tired too." When I got into the feather bed, it felt like I was on a cloud. *This trip just keeps getting better.*

When I woke up, I didn't smell coffee. *What's going on? My dad always has the coffee brewing in the morning.* I went downstairs to see what was going on.

Mary said, "Stay in here with me."

I peeked out the window and saw my father talking to a knight. He looked worried.

The knight got back on his horse and left.

When my dad came back into the house, Mary and I asked him what he wanted.

He said, "They wanted you, Tyler. Someone told them that a beautiful farm girl lived here, and they wanted to know where you were. I told them that you were staying with your grandmother, that she was ill. They are picking up all the single maidens today and tomorrow."

I said, "Father, maybe I should go. Maybe it would be good for me."

"No. You don't want that kind of life. You want true love. I want you to stay close to the house for the next week."

For the next few days, I stayed in the house. Mary and I did a lot of baking. I asked if I could milk the cows.

Mary said, "If you go around the back way, but do not go outside. We can't take a chances if they are watching the house."

I went into the barn and got my bucket and my little stool. While I milked the cows, I noticed the hay moving.

A hand appeared in the hay, and I froze. I didn't know what to do. *Are the knights hiding in the barn?*

A handsome man with wavy hair popped up and said, "Please don't be afraid. I am hiding from the knights. I am wounded, and I need a bandage. Can you help me? I promise I will not hurt you. I just need a place to hide."

I said, "What are you doing?"

He had dark hair and dark eyes. "I was wounded while saving some farm girls from the knights."

I asked, "Do you live around here?"

He said, "No, I'm not from this area. I live far away from here. Don't let anyone know I'm here. You could put your life in jeopardy."

I said, "Let me see your wound. Okay. We need to stitch it up." I got some soap and water, a needle, and some thread. I tore some material from my skirt to use as a bandage.

He looked exactly how I had envisioned my knight in shining-armor would look. I told him my name.

He said, "My name is Miles. Do you mind keeping a secret?"

I said, "I don't mind. Let me get you some food. I'll be right back." I figured I could get some fresh bread and cheese. Mary had left, and father was in his study reading. I knew I wouldn't be noticed in the kitchen. *I believed Miles when he said I could trust him. I wonder what is going to happen in this dream? I am hiding, and he is hiding. This could get exciting.*

Miles had pale skin and the most beautiful features. He reminded me of an angel. *Maybe he is my angel, and he is coming to save me. Oh, that's just great. Now I'm dreaming within a dream. My father would kill me if he knew I was hiding Miles in the barn. My father and I don't have secrets. Ever since my mother died, he and I have been very close. I can tell him anything, and he can tell me anything.*

I thought about Miles while I fell asleep, and I woke up to my husband staring at me.

I said, "What are you doing?"

He said, "You're just lucky I didn't wake you up in the middle of the night. I came very close to disturbing your very peaceful sleep."

I said, "Thanks for letting me sleep." *At least he wants me. What am I going to learn from this dream? I wonder what is going to happen.* I got up to take a shower. I put my shower cap on my head and popped into the shower.

Michael wanted to know why I didn't brush my teeth first because I always brushed my teeth first.

I said, "I don't know. I decided to take a shower first."

He stuck his head in the shower, gave me a kiss, and asked what I would like to do for breakfast.

Mr. Catalfamo called to see if we would like to come over for breakfast before heading back home. We packed our bags, and when we came out of our room, a limo was waiting for us. We had breakfast on their patio, which overlooked their vineyard, and it was absolutely amazing.

Everything these people do is perfect. I love that trait in people. It is a trait I don't possess, but I wish I did.

After breakfast, Michael and Mr. Catalfamo talked about business.

Mrs. Catalfamo and I had coffee in the kitchen. Gloria let me know she liked me, and she was looking forward to my husband handling their account. The kitchen looked like a kitchen in *Better Homes and Gardens*. Huge windows in the back showcased the vineyard.

I said, "Your home is so beautiful. Everything is so perfect."

She said, "Thank you. When we did the renovations, I designed exactly what I wanted."

I said, "Well, it's perfect."

"Thank you. That's why I like you. We have the same taste."

We both giggled.

She said, "We have a case of wine for you to take home. We hope you like it."

"Thank you so much. I'm sure we will love it."

The men came into the kitchen, and Mr. Catalfamo announced that Michael was their new attorney. He couldn't have been happier to have Michael handling their account.

On our way home, Michael and I talked about the kids and what we were going to do for dinner. His tone turned serious, and he said, "I want you to know that I couldn't be more proud to have you as my wife. You have been a wonderful support to me and my career—not to mention a wonderful mother. I appreciate everything you do for our family." He handed me a check for five thousand dollars. "I want you to have this money. I want you to go shopping and enjoy yourself."

I couldn't believe it. It was so unexpected. I was shocked.

He said, "And when we get home, I know you like to get unpacked right away. I'll go get the kids while you unpack and get things in order."

I was still in shock. It made me so happy to know that he truly loved me and that he acknowledged how important I was to him and our family. I felt I had a purpose with him and our family for the first time in a long time. It felt good.

He said, "I'm going to pick up the kids and get takeout from the Chinese restaurant around the corner."

I said, "That sounds great."

He said, "I know you're tired."

He knows me so well.

I got everything unpacked and put away. I put some clothes in the washer and got the dishes ready for dinner. When Michael and the kids got home, we had a really nice dinner. We talked about our weekend, and I loved just being together.

I thought about wearing the sexy negligee, but my comfy pajamas were more appealing. I hugged the kids, kissed Michael good night, and hopped into bed. The cool breeze coming through the window was so relaxing. I went right to sleep.

I woke up in the kitchen. *How am I going to bring food out to Miles without drawing any attention? I'll figure something out. This is very exciting. I'm not just milking cows today.*

Mary had made extra rolls at breakfast, so I hid a few in a napkin. I asked if she could wrap some extra food in cheesecloth so I would have something to nibble on while I was working in the barn.

She said, "I'll be cleaning the windows if you need me. They got muddy from the rain."

I asked if she needed any help.

She said, "No, no. I'll do it."

I was relieved because I wanted to see Miles, but first I needed to see what my father was doing. He was reading in the front room.

I quickly grabbed the food for Miles and went to the barn.

The morning sun was shining through the windows of the barn, but I couldn't see Miles. I wondered if he had left. I looked all over for him, and when he stood up, he startled me.

I didn't realize how big and muscular he was. I was taken aback, but then I got myself together and handed him his coffee and rolls.

He said, "Thank you for everything. Will you sit and talk with me?"

I said, "Of course. I would love to."

We sat on the hay and talked for the longest time.

He told me about himself, where he was from, and how he got here. He had heard horror stories about our king. He wanted to help change the Monarchy.

How is he going do that by himself?

He asked about my life.

I said, "I was born and raised here. My mother had passed away. It's just me and my father now."

My mandolin was sitting near the door. He asked if I played.

I said, "Yes, I play."

"Could you play for me?" he asked.

"Okay, but I don't want anyone to hear."

As I started to get up to get the mandolin, Miles grabbed my hand. He looked at me with a gentle but serious look.

I wasn't nervous. For some reason, I trusted him. I felt no fear.

He asked if I had ever been kissed.

I told him no.

He leaned toward me and kissed me.

All of a sudden, fire shot through my body. I kissed him back. Every part of my body and soul came alive. It was like I had been dead, and I didn't even realize it. We held each other in the hay. I don't think he expected to feel that way either. It was an awakening.

I must have dozed off because I woke up at home.

Michael came in with a cup of coffee and said, "I was thinking about taking the day off. We could spend some time together ... just us. And I thought we could plan that trip to Las Vegas you always wanted to take."

I looked at him with surprise. I said, "What?"

He said, "You have always wanted to go there."

"I know, but I'm wondering why you want to do all this all of a sudden. You need to go to work. You have a lot to do for your new clients. I'll take care of the kids and the house, and we can talk about Las Vegas later, okay?"

He looked at me sweetly and said, "Okay."

After he left, I sat on my bed and wondered what was going to happen with Miles. *It's getting exciting—and so is my real life. I wonder what's going to happen with that too.*

I had a lot to do. My cleaning lady quit, and I hadn't hired a new one because I was hoping my old cleaning girl would come back. *I don't think it's going to happen. It's been a few weeks, and I haven't heard from her. I think it's time to let go. I have a ton to do with organizing and cleaning out closets. I had better get started.*

After working all morning, I decided to lie down on the couch for a few minutes. I woke up in the barn with Miles. I heard horses out in front. We looked at each other, not knowing what to do or where to go.

He looked at me sweetly and said, "Don't be afraid. I'll protect you." He gently kissed my lips.

I said, "How are you going to do this all alone?"

He said, "There are many people involved. I'm leading the uprising. There is someone in this house. Someone in this area is helping me."

My father came into the barn and saw us. I thought he would be upset, but he said, "Miles, you got here. I am so relieved to see you. I didn't think you were going to make it."

My father was helping Miles?

Miles said, "I got here last night."

Father looked at me and said, "Tyler, you didn't tell me he arrived."

"Father, I couldn't. I didn't know how you would react."

"We'll talk later, young lady."

They started to talk about the uprising, and I was not part of the conversation.

The men on the horses were coming into the barn. My father asked me to go get food for the men.

I said, "Will some bread and cheese do?"

He said, "That's perfect. Hurry up now."

When I got back, six other men were in the barn. They all knew my dad and Miles. I was shocked by my dad's involvement in the clandestine revolution, but his courage made me feel proud that he was my father. As I looked around the, I couldn't help but admire the men who were risking their lives for their kingdom and the people they loved. It seemed that everyone had a stake in this uprising except for Miles. *Who is he? And why is he willing to risk his own life for strangers and people of a kingdom he has no claim to? I've never met anyone like him. He is an angel, my angel.*

My father said, "Tyler, why don't you go to bed now. We have a lot to discuss, and it's getting late. We will talk tomorrow, and I'll explain everything."

Miles grabbed my hand and kissed it, sending chills all over my body and melting my heart.

I said good night to everyone and went up to my room. I had pushed my bed against the window so I could look at the stars. The sky was full of them, and I picked the brightest one. I wished for peace in our kingdom and the safety of all the men involved. I also wished that Miles would come back to me just like in my dreams—and we would live happily ever after.

I fell asleep while dreaming about my Prince Charming and woke up on my couch. *I still have a lot of cleaning to do. I better get up. I know the perfect pick-me-up.*

I made a cup of coffee and slowly got back to cleaning and organizing. Whenever I clean and organize my house, I feel a whole lot better.

By the time Michael got home, it was dinnertime. *There is no way this princess is going to cook dinner.* Instead, I ordered Chinese food.

Michael honked the horn, and I went out to the garage. The automatic garage door opener was stuck, and I had to release the door manually.

When Michael came into the house, he was waving two tickets.

I said, "What are you doing?"

He said, "These are two tickets to Las Vegas. They're for you and me, but they will have to wait until I get back."

I said, "Back from where?"

He said, "The Catalfamos want me to fly to Italy to meet with their attorneys there and see their other vineyard."

"Oh my. When are you going?"

He said, "I have to leave tomorrow. I would take you, but it's going to be all business. I wouldn't be able to spend any time with you."

"That's okay. I have to take care of the kids. On this short notice, I couldn't get away anyhow. Besides, this is about you making money for our family, and that's a good thing."

We ate dinner and got to bed early. I told him I would help him pack in the morning. I was exhausted from cleaning all day.

We said good night to the kids and got into bed. *Clean sheets are one of my favorite things in the whole world. Maybe it is a sign that we aren't going to Las Vegas yet. It just seems odd that he would have to go to Italy on such short notice. I wonder how much traveling he will have to do for these clients?*

I woke up with the sun in my eyes. All I could think about was Miles. He was downstairs. I hurried up, got dressed, and went down to the kitchen.

Miles was making coffee.

That's my kind of man.

My dad had to go outside to get the horses ready. He said, "I'll be back in a few minutes."

I thought I would get breakfast started. As I was getting the ingredients out to make the bread, I said, "Miles, what stake do you have in this fight? I don't understand."

He said, "Okay, I'll tell you why I'm here. My mother escaped this area when she was a young girl, the same age as you. She escaped, but many people she knew and loved did not. When she met my father, they fell in love. He happened to be the prince of his kingdom, and as far back as I remember, she told me the story of how she escaped. It still haunts her to see people she loved taken from their families. I vowed to do all I could to free the people of her kingdom and bring peace to their lives. That is why I am here."

"Do you have any siblings?"

"Yes. I have an older brother, and he is to be king when my father passes."

"And you?"

"I am to be king of this kingdom. My mother was a princess in this kingdom before she escaped. This is her domain, and that is why I'm so passionate about this uprising."

Chills went down my spine. I had my back to him while I looked for the flour.

He said, "When I saw you in the barn, I thought you looked like a beautiful flower. I haven't seen anything quite as lovely." He turned me toward him and kissed me.

I got so nervous. I said, "We can't do this. My father will be back at any moment."

He said, "What are you doing?"

I said, "I'm making some fresh rolls for breakfast."

He said, "Let me help."

"Oh no. I can't let a king make the rolls. No way."

He smiled at me, and we giggled.

Father came into the kitchen and said, "Miles, the men have arrived. We have to go."

We stared at each other.

I could tell he didn't want to go—and I didn't want to let him go. I said, "What about breakfast?"

Father said, "We don't have time. We must leave now." He left me strict instructions to stay inside the house. "Do not go outside for anything."

I promised I would stay inside. I hugged them good-bye, and they were off.

I watched out the window as they rode off on their horses. The house was so quiet and eerie. I decided to clean. *Cleaning helps the day go by faster, and I don't get myself thinking too much.* I finished making the rolls, and then I started in the kitchen. Before I knew it, most of the day had passed by—and the house was clean.

I wasn't thinking when I went outside to sweep the dirt off the walkway in front of the house. I didn't hear the knight on a horse behind me.

He said, "You are summoned by the king. Come with me."

I turned around and saw a huge horse and the knight. *What have I done? My father is going be so upset with me. I should run—but where can I go? No, I should fight.*

As he got off his horse, I swung at him with my broom. I kept swinging and swinging. *They are not taking me without a fight.*

I woke up on a pile of hay. I felt dizzy and sick to my stomach. I heard people crying as I looked around. I saw girls holding each other, and they were distraught. I was not altogether there. My head was throbbing as I tried to get myself up. *That knight must have hit me real hard because I have a huge knot on my head.* I couldn't tell where I was, and my vision was blurred. I thought about my father and Miles. *They are going to be worried. I have to get back home.* I passed out thinking of them.

I woke up at home, smelling coffee. This time, my daughter was bringing me a cup.

I said, "Where is Dad?"

"He's getting luggage out of the attic."

I asked her if she made the coffee.

She said, "No, Dad made it. He just asked me to bring you a cup."

"Oh, thank you."

"You're welcome."

I was still a bit dazed from my dream, but everything started coming back to me. *He's packing for Italy. I had better get up and help him. That would be nice.*

My husband came into the bedroom with a few pieces of luggage and said, "Would you like me to bring you something back from my trip?"

I said, "If you have time, but if you don't, it's not important.

The kids were eating breakfast and watching television in the den when we left for the airport. I told them I'd be back in an hour. We got to the airport about an hour before his flight, but I still dropped him off.

When we got out of the car to get his things out of the trunk, he looked at me and said, "You look so beautiful in the morning. It's refreshing to see. I want you to know how lucky I feel to have you in my life. Thank you for standing by me and pushing me forward." He put his index finger on my nose, wiggled my nose, and left.

What has gotten into him?

On the drive home, I started thinking about my dream. *I can't get caught up with that right now. I need to think about the kids and what we are doing today. I think it is going to be a nice day for the beach. Maybe we can have lunch at the beach—that sounds good.*

When I got home, the kids had their bathing suits on and were ready to go.

I said, "Give me a few minutes while I change."

It's funny how you become friends with your kids as they get older. I feel like I have two best friends. It's fun. We had a great day at the beach, and we grabbed sandwiches for lunch. We laughed all day long, which was a pleasant surprise.

On the way home, I stopped at the grocery store and picked up some appetizers. When we got home, we took showers and watched a movie together. By bedtime, we were all tired. *The sun has a way of draining your energy.*

I opened my window to get some fresh air. I looked up at the bright shining stars. I love a starry night. I thought about Michael's layover in New York. I crawled into bed and awoke in a dungeon.

I was rubbing my head. I heard crying, and when I looked to see who it was, I noticed about twenty girls in the dungeon. One of the knights brought us some stale rolls and some dirty water. *How do they expect us to eat these hard rolls and drink this contaminated water?*

The girls looked like they were starving, and they ate and drank like they'd never seen food. They said they had been there for days without any food or water. They said they had been treated like animals.

The knight yelled, "The king is going to summon you to his court sometime today."

After he left, more knights came down to the dungeon.

It seemed so surreal as I was trying to get myself together. I was thinking about my dad and how angry he was going to be with me for going outside. I knew that Miles would save me.

Meanwhile, back at the cottage, my father and Miles discovered a broken broom on the front walkway and one of my slippers on the ground. They could tell that something terrible had happened—and that I had been taken against my will.

Both Miles and my father knew there was no time to waste. The king and his court are ruthless.

I told the girls to calm down, that everything was going to be all right, and that we were going to be saved. *How do I know we are going to be all right? It's a dream. Of course I'm going be all right. Everyone will be all right, I hope.*

Six more knights arrived. They were claiming their girls by putting bracelets on the ones they wanted. My father was right. They were not at all what I had imagined in my dreams. They were rude and aggressive. There was nothing romantic about how we were treated.

Someone yelled, "The king is coming."

One of the knights looked at me and said, "I'll have her."

I said, "I'm not yours to have," and I kicked him.

He grabbed me and tried to put his bracelet on my wrist.

I said, "Leave me alone." *There is no way I am going to let him claim me. I'd rather die than have someone treat me like some sort of object that they own.*

The king entered the cell. "Leave her," he said. "She is mine. Find someone else to claim for your own."

He looked upset as he turned and walked away. The king left instructions with the key master to send me to the maid's quarters where they would clean me up. The next thing I knew, I was being taken away. As I was leaving, I looked at the girls and said, "Don't worry. We are going to be saved."

The maid's quarters were beautiful—a far cry from the dungeon. The girls or maidens were there to help get me ready for the king. Some of them had been there for a year or two, serving the king and his knights in any fashion they desired. I was horrified to think of being held in the castle as a servant to the king and his court.

Someone came into our room to let them know the king was ready for me. They rushed to get me dressed. It was the most beautiful dress I had ever seen—and made of the finest materials—but I couldn't let them dress me. I ran from them.

They said, "Please. If we don't have you ready for the king when they come to get you, we will be punished." They pleaded with me until I submitted to their wishes. They thanked me for understanding as they finished dressing me.

When they were done, a guard came into the maid's quarters to get me. He didn't come get me like a gentleman; he grabbed me in a very abusive manner.

My first reaction was to get away from him. I tried to escape while the door was open. He came after me, brought me back into the maid's quarters, and threw me onto some pillows.

I must have hit my head again because I passed out and woke up to the morning sun shining through my window. The smell of coffee did not permeate through the house like every other morning. *Where is my coffee? That's right. Michael is in Italy.*

I popped up, put a robe on, and made the coffee. I wondered if Michael had made it to Italy yet and how his flight was.

Just then, the phone rang. It was Michael. He had arrived late the night before and woke up at two o'clock in the afternoon. He said, "I wish you were here. The city is beautiful. I had a meeting with the attorneys for the Catalfamos. I'm absolutely going to bring you a gift."

I said, "Don't worry about me. Just do what you have to do— and have fun even though you are working."

He said, "I have to get ready. The meeting is at three o'clock. I love you, and I'll call you later."

I am glad I talked to him first thing this morning. Now I can go about my day without worrying about him.

I was sipping on my coffee and watching the news when the phone rang again. My girlfriend wanted to know if I would like to have lunch at the mall.

I said, "That sounds perfect. I'll meet you in front of Bloomingdale's at noon."

I finished my coffee, got some things done around the house, took a shower, and got dressed.

The kids needed a ride to a friend's house. It would be perfect if I could drop them off before noon.

When I parked in front of Bloomingdale's, I saw my girlfriend. We looked at each other and giggled. We got out of our cars and hugged. We decided to eat lunch before we went shopping.

We ate at the bar in an Italian restaurant and caught up on our lives.

Her life was getting better, and she was much happier. She hadn't been dreaming as much as a result.

I said, "Not me. I'm still dreaming. In fact, I am caught up in one right now—and it's starting to get very exciting."

She said, "You will have to keep me informed."

"Michael is in Italy."

"I'm surprised you didn't go with him. It's so beautiful there. You must go with him next time." She grabbed the check when the waiter brought it and insisted on treating me to lunch.

I said, "Only if I get to treat next time."

She said, "It's a deal."

We laughed.

After lunch, we went shopping. I picked up a few things for the kids and bought myself a really cute outfit. It was a fun day. I was glad she called.

She said, "Keep in touch. I miss seeing you. My life is getting better—I hope yours does too." We hugged each other and said good-bye.

When I got home, the house was empty and quiet. I turned on the television so I wouldn't feel so alone. The kids called and said they were going to be home at ten o'clock. For dinner, I didn't feel like cooking. Instead, I made a sandwich and watched television before bed.

I opened the window to get a better night's sleep.

When I woke up, the king said, "Where is she?"

The maids told him what had happened.

He said, "Bring her to me when she wakes up."

I kept my eyes closed until the king left.

One of the girls pointed at me and said, "You are very lucky."

Another girl was giggling because she knew I was pretending to be asleep.

I asked them why I was brought to the castle.

They said I was going to be a servant to the king just as they had been.

One of the girls said, "We are the lucky ones. The others are treated a lot worse. We at least have good food and beautiful clothes to wear. It's not what we dreamed about, but it could be much worse."

Guards rushed past our door, and the king said, "Close the gates."

We looked out the window and saw men on horses carrying torches. They were riding close to each other as a strong, united force. Most of the men got across the drawbridge before it closed.

We couldn't believe what was happening. One of the girls screamed, "Maybe we are going to be rescued!"

Maybe Miles and my father are here. Yes, we are going to be rescued!

One of the guards came into our quarters and said, "Stay inside this room. Don't come out."

I sat in the corner and prayed that Miles and my father were coming.

I dozed off again and woke up at home. I made coffee and thought about the time change in Italy. *It's got to be about noon there. It's strange that everyone doesn't live in the same time zone.*

I was excited because the kids and I were going to dinner and then a a musical. I was looking forward to it. When I was young, I loved musicals and Broadway plays. *Godspell* was my favorite. I hadn't thought about that play in forever, I loved the music, and I especially loved the song "Day by Day."

I am very blessed. I have wonderful memories of childhood, and I hope my kids have wonderful memories as well. I love when I remember the simple things that make me happy because sometimes I forget. Out of the blue, a simple memory reminds me of something all over again. It puts a smile on my face—even if it's just a glimpse of a memory. Music can evoke a certain time in life; it inspires me, saddens me, and reminds me of the rainbow of emotions that life brings.

I'm so happy my daughter wants to be a singer.

When we are children, we are more aware of the things we love. Life is simpler, but as we get older, we lose perspective and get caught up in the wrong things. Life happens, and we forget how to be happy.

The kids and I will grab an early dinner before the show. I think they are excited about going. My daughter has been listening to the soundtrack of Mamma Mia *all week, which is what we are going to see.*

The musical was wonderful, and both kids really enjoyed it. I was happy that they loved it as much as I did. On the way home, my husband called us.

I said, "Honey, what time is it there. Shouldn't you be sleeping?"

He said he couldn't seem to get into the rhythm of the time change, but it didn't matter because he was coming home tomorrow. "I miss you," he said. "I got you a gift. I think you will like it. In fact, I know you will."

I said, "Don't tell me what you got for me. Let it be a surprise. I like surprises. We miss you too and can't wait to see you. Have a safe flight home."

When we got home, the kids went to bed. I ended up taking a relaxing bubble bath before bed. I went into a deep sleep instead of tossing and turning.

I woke up to screaming. I wondered if my father and Miles would find me.

The king and a guard came into our quarters and grabbed me.

When they grabbed another girl, she tried to get away. The guard hit her, and blood trickled down her face.

They are in no mood. I had better go along with them and not do anything rash.

There was a beautiful tapestry on the wall that went down to the ground. Behind it, there was a door that brought us to a secret passageway. When we went through the secret passage, I turned and saw my father. I yelled to him, but the guard closed the door. The damp corridor led us out to a huge boat.

If we get on that boat, how can they save us?

We went out into the open water. It was like the ocean. I looked back at the castle. As we were drifting away, I started crying. *I'll never see them again.* The castle looked like an inferno.

The king said, "I'm going to go back one day and regain my kingdom."

I hope Miles regains the kingdom for his mother. Through the fire and smoke, another ship was coming at us. My heart dropped, and I hoped it was Miles.

The king ordered the guard to lock us up below.

He threw us in a dark, rat-infested room. *I'm not going in there.*

He threw me so hard against the wall that I passed out again.

I woke up thinking about Michael. He was returning from Italy that night, and I wanted to clean the house and make a special dinner. I had a lot to do. The laundry was in piles, and I wanted to clean all the linens. I hopped out of bed, made some coffee, and got moving.

At two o'clock, I started to think about dinner. *Steak, mashed potatoes with celery root, and a bottle of pinot noir from the vineyard of his new clients will be perfect. I also want to get some fresh flowers for the table.* I was excited. I set the table beautifully and got everything ready before I picked him up at the airport. I put on a cute outfit, fixed my hair, and put a little makeup on. I wanted to look good.

I got to the airport and parked in a no-parking zone. Luckily, the security guard allowed me to park there for a few minutes. I even got luckier when I saw Michael walking out toward the car. He looked so handsome. I was glad to see him. I didn't realize how much I had actually missed him until then. I popped the trunk and jumped out to give him a hug.

He grabbed me and said, "I wished I had roses to shower you with, but instead, I have perfume."

I love perfume. I was happy that he took the time and thought about me. I told him about the steaks, and he was happy that we were going to stay home for dinner. He was exhausted from the time change and flying.

When we got home, I made him a drink while he got changed.

He insisted on grilling the steaks.

I said, "I thought you might feel that way."

When it was time for bed, he said, "I love you, but I have to go bed. I am beat."

I was glad. I wanted to take a hot bubble bath and relax. It had been a long day. After my bath, I got into bed and fell right to sleep.

I woke up on hay that reeked of rodents.

A girl was wiping my face saying, "Wake up. Please wake up."

Where am I?

We were in a jail cell. We could see through the wrought-iron bars. We noticed the keys hanging on a nail. We looked around for something that would help us fetch the keys. I found a stick in the haystack that was long enough to reach.

We retrieved the keys and opened the cell door.

The girl was crying, and I asked what was wrong. I said, "We got out."

She said, "I know, but I'm frightened of the water. I can't swim."

I said, "Don't worry. It will be okay. Just follow me very closely up the stairs."

When we got up to the top of the stairs, it was total pandemonium. Everybody was running around in all directions, and we were lucky that nobody was paying any attention to us. We hid behind some barrels of rum.

There was fighting all around us. The men from the other ship were boarding ours.

I looked around for my father and Miles. When I got a quick glance of Miles, my heart sank—and I got the chills.

Miles yelled my name.

Without thinking, I got up.

At that moment, the king put his sword against my neck.

Miles said, "Let her go."

The king said, "No!"

Miles was not giving up on me. He said, "What do you want?"

The king said, "I want a safe way out of here."

Miles said, "All right. We will set you up with a boat and one man.

The king said, "I heard you were a man of your word."

I thought, *I love a man of his word.*

Once everything was set up, the king threw me to the ground and left with his knight.

Miles helped me up and kissed me. His lips were soft and gentle, and it wasn't just any kiss. It was special. He was special— and the feeling between us was special.

He said, "We are going to stay on the ship tonight. Some of the men will take the prisoners back on the other ship. I heard this ship has the most beautiful captain's quarters. We can talk and catch up with each other there. Nobody will bother us." He winked at me and smiled.

I said, "What about my father?"

He said, "Your father knows you are with me."

We went to the captain's quarters, and we talked for a long time.

There was a knock at the door, and several men brought in trays of food and wine. They set everything up.

Miles looked at me and smiled because he knew I was surprised.

We ate, drank, and talked. It felt like we had been together for our entire lives. It was so comfortable, and it was so right.

I started to yawn, and Miles came over and held out his hand. I grabbed his hand and stood up.

He lifted me up and brought me over to the bed gently.

I closed my eyes while he rubbed my back and my legs. He was very gentle and loving. He even rubbed my head. I opened my eyes and looked at him. He grabbed me and held me. As we made love, I couldn't help but remember all my dreams, all the men who loved me, and all the men I loved.

When we were done, Miles looked at me and said, "First time, huh?"

I just looked at him and smiled.

We fell asleep in each other's arms.

When I woke up, I felt a fresh breeze flowing through my window and smelled fresh-brewed coffee. *Oh my, what a perfect morning!*

Michael walked in with breakfast and a square box on a tray.

Another present? But he got me perfume. What could this be? I looked at him and said, "What's this?"

Michael said, "Just open it."

When I opened it, I could hardly believe what I saw. It was a gorgeous ruby-and-diamond bracelet. I said, "Oh my. Oh my." I looked at him with such adoration. Michael really thought about me and what I like—the window, the fresh coffee, the perfume, and the jewelry—and he made me feel so special and so loved.

He said, "I have one more thing to show you." He showed me a check for $100,000. "It's a bonus from the firm. I know there are a lot of things you want, including a new home."

I replied, "I don't want a new home. I love this house." *What have I done to deserve all this attention?*

"I have to run around and get some things done. I'll be back this afternoon. I want you to relax and watch some television. Do whatever you want."

I said, "Thank you."

After he left, I cleaned up a little, turned on the television, and dozed off on the couch.

Miles was still holding me and looking at me.

I turned to him and said, "What are you looking at?"

He said, "A beautiful princess. I want you to be in my life forever. I never want to let you go." He gently took my face in his hands and started to kiss my face, neck, and ears. His lips were so soft, and his touch was even softer. He made me feel like I was on a cloud.

After we made love, we got dressed in our underclothes because we wanted to go for a swim. We jumped into the water and swam around.

He grabbed me and whispered, "This is the happiest I've ever been."

I looked at him, smiled, and said, "Me too."

We got dressed and headed back.

My father and some other men were waiting for us near the castle.

Miles went to my father and told him what had happened to the king. He said, "They aren't going to make it."

My father said, "Miles, I'm afraid there was a leak in the boat. While I was looking through my spyglass, I could see their small boat accumulating water. It must have been his fate. The king is gone."

Miles said, "That's not the most important thing I want to discuss with you, though. I want to ask for your daughter's hand in marriage.

My father was elated. He said, "Yes. I would be proud to have you as my son."

We walked through the kingdom. People up and down the street cheered for Miles because they knew the king was gone.

I waved to the girl who'd helped me in the castle and on the ship.

Miles went up to the balcony of the castle and announced our marriage plans.

The next thing I knew, I was in a huge cathedral—and I was wearing the most beautiful wedding gown.

My father walked me down the aisle, and Miles smiled at me with the most loving look in his eyes.

That night, in the royal quarters, we made love. *I have never felt such peace and such love in all my life. I am home to stay. I've found my noble king.*

I held my husband and fell asleep—and then I woke up.

Author's Note

જી

For as far back as I can remember, I have been a dreamer. I wrote *Mia* during the loneliest time in my life. The emptiness was so great that I sometimes thought I would go insane. In desperation, to escape my sadness, I turned to my dreams for comfort. That comfort lifted my spirits and got me through the darkest hours of my life. Cause Lord only knows my real story was no fairy tale.

My hope is that *Mia* might help someone who feels trapped in an unhappy relationship and feels like there is no way out. It's for people who are waiting for "the one" to come into their lives and take them away. We can find a way to escape—even if just for a short time.

My dreams saved me from making mistakes that I would have regretted, and those dreams became my salvation.

My wish for you is that your dreams can save you and become your salvation by giving light where there is darkness, by giving love where there is emptiness, and by giving hope where there is hopelessness. You too can move forward toward a better day.

Thanks for dreaming with me.

Printed in the United States
By Bookmasters